TWISTED KNIGHT

Omerta

R.G. ANGEL

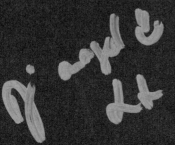

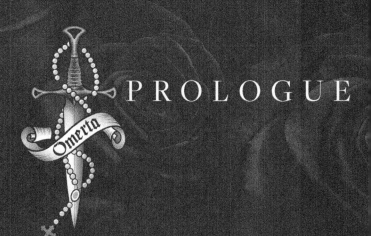

"Father, why now?" I tried to sound blasé despite the fear building in the pit of my stomach as I looked at the blond girl crouched in the corner of the window-less room.

She was sobbing, her face buried in her folded knees, but she couldn't be much older than my thirteen years.

My father's ever-present scowl deepened. "Because I told you to. Because it's time for you to become a man. Because this girl needs breaking before we sell her."

A wave of nausea hit me. My mother had kept me as far away from my father's side business, too scared of who I would become, a replica of him. Faithless, immoral, evil.

But she had died a year ago and I was now at his mercy. How many times had I wanted to tell the truth to Luca? My friend despite being the son of a low-grade made man and him being Mafia royalty, but what then? I'd have my father's death and the one of all his men on my conscience, and what if what he did had been allowed? I'd be a traitor and what would they do to me?

I was just a boy, a coward who was nothing more than a lackey to his father.

I looked at the girl again. She peeked at me through her curtain of blond hair, her blue eyes filled with tears and dread.

"I don't want to."

My father punched me, and I tasted the blood in my mouth as I fell heavily to the floor.

"Very well then, she'll have you to thank for what she will go through. You'll stay and watch." He pressed a button and three of my father's men walked in.

The first one was a six-foot-seven three-hundred-pound man they called The Monster. He looked at the girl with a sick glimpse in his eyes.

"These three or you. Your choice."

The girl looked up and paled before turning toward me, her eyes almost begging.

How could this poor girl beg me to hurt her?

I sighed with defeat. "I'll do it."

My father clasped his hand on my shoulder. "I knew you'd do the right thing, son."

I moved toward the girl and undressed her as she

cried, my hand shaking under my father's scrutiny. What a way for this poor girl to lose her virginity. I'd lost mine a couple months ago on my thirteenth birthday to a prostitute twice my age. Not really the way I had wanted, but nothing like what that poor girl was about to go through.

"It'll be okay," I whispered to her, hoping my father was too far away to hear and would not take this for kindness or weakness which we both would pay for. "What's your name?"

"Emily," she sobbed as I pulled her toward the bed and unzipped my pants, trying to block out everything around us—my father's sadistic eyes and what I was doing to her.

I closed my eyes and entered her as gently as I could, trying to make less of the nightmare it must have been for her, and as I thrust into her, her sobs turned to wails and as I stole her innocence, I felt the little I had left vanished too.

It was the day I lost my soul and part of my humanity... And it had only been the beginning of my hell.

1

D O M

Twenty years later

"Please, no, don't!" she shouted, trying to crawl away from me. "I beg you, don't hurt me."

I growled, her fear resonating all the way to my cock, making it harder than steel.

I pulled at her legs and wrapped my hand around her neck, squeezing hard as I slammed my cock inside her.

She thrashed with every thrust, tried to claw at my face. I let go of her throat, and she took a sharp breath as I grabbed her wrists with one hand.

"Please don't," she sobbed as I slammed into her harder.

She cried out with every ruthless thrust. I closed my eyes, grunting, losing myself in the moment.

I came hard and as soon as I was done, I stood up as the now familiar wave of self-loathing filled me.

I discarded my condom and zipped my pants, smoothing my features before turning toward her.

"You took acting lessons?" I asked, lighting a cigarette, looking at her lying on the bed with a little satisfied smile on her face.

She gave me a half smile. "You're not supposed to smoke in here."

I snorted. "I'm sure Genevieve will let that one slide."

Genevieve Dupont, the Madame of The Rectory, owed the *famiglia* a lot for so many things; we were basically kings here.

She extended her hand. "Then give me a smoke. I think I earned it."

I extended her the cigarette; she took a puff. "And yes, I did take some classes. A lot of guys are into the same things as you are. Your kinks are not that special. The only thing that is different here is that I have a hard time pretending I'm not coming with you because your big dick really hit my G-spot."

I nodded, grabbing the cigarette back from her. There was a difference between those guys and me. For them it was just a kink, an itch to scratch, some rough play they couldn't bring home to the wife, but for me it was different.

I was a monster, a sick bastard. For me it was the only way to get it up, her screams and her fighting that made me come.

I got out a wad of bills out of my pocket and threw five hundred dollars on her nightstand.

She looked at the money and threw me a sultry look. "The going rate is three hundred fifty dollars."

I shrugged, grabbing my jacket from the red velvet chair in the corner. "Bonus for all your hard work."

Elodie was the only prostitute at The Rectory that enjoyed the fight and the all non-con play so she was the only woman I picked because contrary to popular belief, I didn't want to hurt women or traumatize them; that was the last thing I wanted to do, despite the monster lurking under the surface, the evil running in my blood... I never wanted to hurt them. It just seemed to be the only way for me to work my cock.

I might have been Mafia, but I still had a conscience, some sort of moral compass—admittedly a misdirected one sometimes, but I lived by my rules.

"Coming back to see me soon?" she asked sultrily, opening her legs in an invitation to repeat what we'd just done.

I sighed. I knew it was going to come eventually; she was misconstruing my repeated visits for attraction or even worse... affection. The only reason I picked her every time was because she enjoyed the depravity instead of enduring it as the others would. How she looked or who she was didn't matter at all to me.

"I'm quite busy," I replied evasively. It was not a lie; my consigliere job was taking a lot of time, especially since Cassie, Luca's wife and my sister at heart, was getting closer to her due date.

Luca was more and more the doting husband and future father than capo these days, and I was making sure I didn't let something slip. I had their backs —always.

Plus, I didn't enjoy sex like that. No, truly I didn't; it was just the only way I could. It was a part of me I hated. I'd be celibate if I could, like Luca did for over two years, but I was not Luca, and my dick sometimes got the better of me despite how shitty and disgusted I felt afterward. That was why I tried to limit my visit to once a month.

"You're an important man." She nodded before sighing and stretching, flaunting her erect nipples to my face. "What if you moved me to your home? You could have me any way you want, every night."

I let out a low chuckle. "You couldn't handle me every night." I was much too rough, much too violent just... too much.

She winked at me. "You'd be surprised."

I was just done with this conversation. I wanted to go home and be with my circle, my family.

"I'll see you around," I said, adjusting my jacket.

I didn't look back at her as I exited the room and walked down the corridor full of doors to other rooms. No matter the pretense of luxury, The Rectory was nothing more than a brothel, but one that valued secrecy above all else and one that will always be here—too many powerful men were part of this exclusive club.

I reached the underground parking and climbed in my gray Porsche 718 Boxster, the only extravagant expense I ever made with the Mafia money I made.

As soon as I turned on my phone, I was assaulted by texts, mostly from Cassie sweet-talking me into stopping at the fast-food joint on my way home.

She had the weirdest cravings during her pregnancy and Luca was all about health kicks. If she shamelessly begged me for that, it was clearly because her husband, my capo, refused but I was a sucker for that woman and even if I knew Luca would shit a brick I was going to stop for her extra-large fries, her burger with extra pickles, and her chocolate milkshake… consequences be damned.

———

"Dom?" she called as soon as I walked in.

I looked down at the greasy, smelly bag I held in

my hand. I swear her pregnancy turned her into a hound.

I went to the kitchen, putting the bag on the table before going to the living room she'd transformed a few months ago.

Cassie had been transforming this austere house with her light; it was nothing like it was just a year ago.

I leaned against the doorframe and looked at her sitting in the fancy pregnancy chair Luca bought her, her hair in a messy bun on top of her head, her pregnancy dress wrapped around her huge stomach.

I smiled tenderly at her. I was home now; I'd left the darkness behind at The Rectory.

"Food's in the kitchen."

She looked up, her face lighting up with a huge smile.

"Domenico, you are the best of men!"

I chuckled. "Let's not say that to your husband, okay?"

She shrugged with a little pout. "He said no."

I laughed again. "I figured."

"Oh!" She rested her hand on the side of her stomach. "The babies are thankful too." She gestured me forward. "Come, you can feel a heel."

I looked down at my hands. I had to shower; no way I was touching her after what I'd done with Elodie, after the impulse I had after I degraded that woman...

I shook my head. "I'm just going to take a quick shower."

She rolled her eyes. "Don't be silly. Here." She pressed her forefinger against a little bump I could see on the side of her stomach.

I pointed toward the kitchen. "You better go eat your greasy food before your husband finds out."

She muttered something under her breath as she pressed the button at the side of her chair to help herself up.

I looked down, trying to hide my grin. Food was the best way to derail her.

"I'll be back in a bit," I told her as she waddled slowly out of the room.

She raised her hand in a dismissive gesture, like she couldn't care less, and right now I was pretty sure that was the case; she was hangry.

I got to my room on the first floor and took a quick shower before going to the second floor to Luca's office.

I knocked once, not really in the mood of exasperating him tonight.

I heard papers shuffling. "Come in."

I opened the door and saw him breathe out a little breath of relief.

"Oh, it's you." He leaned back on his chair, ignoring the papers in front of him. "Come in."

I walked in and leaned forward, peeking at his

computer screen and the medical article on twin pregnancy.

I shook my head and looked at the empty glass on his desk. "Want a refill?"

He nodded, turning toward the screen again and rubbing his chin; it was something he did when he was preoccupied.

"She's going to be fine," I said as I served us both a double drink.

He sighed. "Yea…" His statement lacked conviction.

"Why are you even hiding up here as your wife is watching her romcom downstairs?"

He rolled his eyes. "I did have some work to do but then—" He shrugged. "She keeps trying to guilt me into getting her some junk food. I already caved four times this week… no more."

"You can go down now; she won't harass you again."

Luca looked heavenward. "You bought her that damn burger, didn't you?"

I nodded. "Of course I did."

"Dom," he started with a weary sigh.

I took a sip of my drink. "You know I'll never refuse her anything."

He rolled his eyes. "It's not good for her."

"She's pregnant, Luca. She's not sick."

"She's so small."

"Yes, and you've put two babies in her. This one's

on you." I meant it as a joke but as Luca paled ever so slightly, I realized he was scared.

I'd rarely seen my best friend scared before. He was the beast capo, the scarred Mafia boss that terrified our rank almost as much as Genovese, the heartless bastard capo dei capi, did, and he was scared now.

"Women have been doing this for thousands of years. She is strong and valiant, our Cassie." I let out a humorless chuckle. "Hell, she would have run a long time ago if it wasn't the case."

"I know." He nodded. "It's just—" He looked toward the computer again, remaining silent.

And I understood exactly everything he was not saying. Cassie was his everything; she had been the one who got him out of his pit of despair and self-destruction. He was living for her, breathing for her. If he'd lost her— I shivered. He would not survive it and I couldn't even blame him.

I used this opportunity to change the subject. "You know, maybe it's not the best time for Cassie's cousin to come."

"Dom... please."

"Luca, as your consigliere—"

Luca laughed. "You know for a title you didn't want, you use that card a lot."

It was not that I didn't *want* to be his consigliere, of course I did, but he was Mafia royalty. I'd been a son of a prostitute and a made man. A made man that was killed in mysterious circumstances when I was fifteen, circumstances that had never been investigated—because everyone, including me, were way too pleased for his untimely death. Luca's position had already been challenged, but I shouldn't have expected anything else from him. What Luca Montanari wanted, he got.

"She's a stranger, Luca. An outsider."

"So was Cassie, and look how she fits in. How much you care for her." He arched an eyebrow. "I mean, in any other circumstances and were you any other man, I would shoot you just for how fusional you two are."

I sighed. "It's different."

"Different how?"

I shook my head. I had no real argument except that we got very lucky with Cassie. Genovese accepted an outsider because Luca had something he wanted and gave it to him in exchange. We also got lucky that Cassie was basically the most caring woman in the world and accepted our darkness without blinking, which was also due to the fact that her parents had been serial killers and so much worse than we could ever be—at least in her eyes.

"Dom, I did all the searches on that woman, plus all the ones you requested." He threw his hands up in exasperation. "I even had the poor woman followed by a PI for days! My wife would kill me for that. She's her family."

I crossed my arms on my chest. I knew I'd lost, not that my argument made a lot of sense to start with.

"Maybe she can come later? Cassie is not due for another month. The woman doesn't know anything about our world; we don't need to risk her discovering who we are."

Luca tapped his fingers rhythmically on his desk. I was getting on his nerves—that was clear.

"She will not go full term." He sighed, rubbing his hands on his face with weariness.

I frowned. "She told me everything was fine with the doctor today."

Luca leaned back on his chair. "And it is but the babies are big and the chances of getting to term are very low. She is scared, Dom. She's putting on a brave face for me and you and the kiddo but it's not enough. She needs a woman by her side, someone who can understand better than we do. Nazalie is sweet but she's not her family and if it makes her feel happy? Safe?" He shrugged. "I'm going to welcome her with open arms."

I didn't expect that. Cassie didn't seem scared of anything, but she was a young woman who went through a lot of things in such a short period of time, so I sometimes forgot she was not a warrior.

I nodded with defeat. "Fine."

"You'll go pick her up? No tricks?"

I rolled my eyes. "I'll be there."

Luca's eyes narrowed in suspicion. "No scaring her so she'd want to leave."

It was a tactic that did cross my mind, but I knew that if the woman told Cassie, she would kick my ass into next week. "I won't."

He nodded, apparently satisfied by my answer. He looked at the clock. "Okay, time to go hunt for my wife. I think I gave her enough time to eat her food and hide the evidence."

I raised an eyebrow, a small smile tugging at my lips. "You won't tell her you know."

He shook his head, a glint of humor in his eyes as he slid a box of tums in his jacket pocket. "No, it makes her way too happy when she thinks she outsmarted me, and I love seeing her happy." He patted his pocket where he put the Tums. "So, I'll be there with her in a couple of hours when she'll start moaning about the heartburn, and I'll be her Tums hero—pretending to not know she did exactly what she was not supposed to."

"That's cute," I admitted.

Luca shrugged. "I love her."

That statement alone was enough. We didn't love often in the Mafia; it could get way too messy. Most Mafia men were in arranged marriages, based on so many factors, and they were not unhappy. We could say that most of them had affection for their wives. But there were a few lucky ones, or unlucky ones, all depending on your views on love, that fell in love hard—like Luca did—and once we loved, it was all-consuming, overbearing at times and forever. It took a strong woman to deal with our kind of love, and Cassie was just that—she was Luca's everything.

These two were a relationship goal; too bad I was way too messed up to ever have a chance to get that.

INDIA

I jolted awake as the plane touched the ground and I looked around groggily. The flight only lasted five hours, but I didn't have the best night and after Cassie's husband, Luca, upgraded me to first class I had to admit that the nap had been heaven.

Once the plane landed, I waited for first class to be emptied before I stood up and reached for my overhead luggage. I always tried to wait for most people to be gone because I had never been keen on the looks I was getting. Some surprised, some judgy, some appreciative... some envious and it had been like that since middle school. I always preferred being invisible, but it was not easy when you were a six-foot-tall woman.

I was genuinely happy that Cassie's and Jude's lives turned around and that she met a lovely man I had yet to meet.

I was also grateful she wanted me to visit; leaving Calgary was a good idea after the breakup. It was not just a normal breakup either. No, it was a destructive bomb, and this chance to get away had been my saving grace. Leaving, even if just for a little while, had been mandatory for my mental health.

I picked up my suitcase and exited the arrival to the sea of people waiting for their friends or family.

It had always been fascinating to me to see people interact at airport arrivals; it had even been the subject of my thesis.

My eyes stopped on a tall, broad man with a well-trimmed goatee. He was studying the crowd too, with a scowl on his face. I sighed when I noticed his sign, 'I. McKenna.' Of course, the boogeyman dressed all in black was here for me.

I stopped in front of him and looked up. That was also quite a rare occurrence too. I was a six-foot-tall woman and meeting taller guys was quite a challenge.

How many guys on dating websites said they were over six feet and weren't? A scarily high number.

"Did the *Men in Black* send you?" I asked with a little grin, trying to lighten the mood and ease the scowl that made me uncomfortable. I had enough experience with angry men; they made me very nervous.

The man looked at me silently, his brown eyes so dark they looked bottomless. He was extremely good-looking, that much was sure, with his square jaw, high cheekbones, and long straight nose. He was not classically good-looking but the dangerous kind —the kind that will burn your heart and soul and leave you breathless and heartbroken in your bed, the kind of man I needed to stay away from. I didn't come for this; I came to stay away from any complications.

"Let's go," he ordered with a low sexy voice before reaching for my suitcase on the floor and walking out.

Was he a security guy working for Cassie's husband? I knew she married well, but I didn't know much more. She'd been quite evasive about the whole situation, but she seemed genuinely happy when I saw her on Skype, so I was not really worried. My cousin had been to hell and back—I trusted her judgment.

"Can I have your name?" I asked the man as we reached the underground parking.

"Domenico."

My pace faltered; it was impossible. *"You* are Dom?" *The* Dom Cassie described to me was funny and kind and all in all a unicorn, but right now he seemed more like a strict asshole to me.

He threw me a side-glance before stopping by a luxurious black car.

"Why?"

I sighed with exasperation. "Are you the type of man to answer questions with another question?"

"And what type of man is that?" he asked, putting my suitcase in the trunk.

I rolled my eyes and followed him to the front of the car.

He reached for a paper from under his wiper; his nostril flared as he read it and looked around the quiet parking lot. If I thought, he was scowling before, he looked murderous now.

"Are you okay?"

"Why wouldn't I be?" he asked, bunching the paper in his fist before putting it in his pocket. "Get in."

"You know it's bound to get very old, very fast," I told him as he reversed the car out of the spot.

"What is?" he asked, throwing me a quick look before concentrating on the road again.

"You!" I snapped. "I met you ten minutes ago, and I already feel like murdering you. Cassie made it seem like you were such a nice person." I shook my head, looking out the window, deciding I was done with him and this conversation.

"Are you really Cassie's cousin?" he asked after a while.

I turned toward him. "Why? Is it the skin color that throws you off?" I was biracial and it's true that when people heard my name McKenna, they rarely expected a half Indian girl to walk in.

"No." He threw me a look that seemed to say it was the stupidest thing he ever heard. "Why would you say that?"

I raised an eyebrow at him; how could I not?

He shook his head. "No, Cassie's a midget."

"And I'm not?"

"Exactly."

I shrugged. "Genetics, I guess. My mom is pale and short like Cassie so I presume it all comes from my father—not that I would know."

"Uh, the joy of genetics."

"Indeed."

I didn't miss the fact that he didn't press the issue about my father—yep, the man knew more about me than he said.

"Let's start over. I wouldn't want Cassie to think I was rude," he said as we exited the interstate.

"But you were."

He threw me an irritated side-look. "Hence the due over."

"You don't want to upset her?"

He snorted. "It won't upset her; it will piss her off and she is even angrier these days."

I laughed at that. "Hormones."

"Terrifying."

I sighed. "Fine, let's start over. Cassie told me you're her best friend."

He nodded, his face softening as a tender smile appeared on his face. I didn't need to be a psychologist to know he really loved my cousin. "I think calling us best friends is a bit basic. It's deeper than that. I love her like my sister, just like I love Luca like my brother."

"And you don't like the idea of a person you don't know coming around and disturbing the dynamic."

He remained silent; it was confirmation enough.

"Occupational hazard. I'll stay out of your way and out of your head."

He nodded once. "It's better for you, trust me. You wouldn't want to roam in there," he said, tapping the side of his head with his forefinger. "You'll come out traumatized," he added with a laugh, but I didn't need to know the man to see he meant it, which made me want to look in it now. Pandora's box was my weakness.

All the thoughts of the complicated man beside me vanished when we passed the iron gate of a gigantic Victorian Manor.

"What is Luca doing for a living again?" I asked, not able to remove my eyes from the place.

"Business," he replied evasively, stopping the car at the bottom of the stone steps.

He got out first and retrieved my bags from the trunk as I waited at the bottom of the steps, looking up at the structure.

"Come," he ordered as he took the first step. "I know Cassie is eager to see you."

I didn't even get a chance to look around the hall as Cassie came out from a room waddling toward me with a wide grin on her face.

"India!" she squealed and I couldn't help but laugh.

I'd not seen my cousin in over three years, and I'd forgotten how short she really was. Now almost at terms with twins she almost looked as wide as she was tall, but despite her obvious discomfort she seemed happy to see me.

"I'm so happy you came."

I leaned down, giving her an awkward hug. "I'm so happy you asked me to come. How are the little ones doing?" I asked, resting my hand on her stomach.

She grinned, resting her hand on top of mine. "Restless and stubborn, like their father." She looked up at me and blinked. "Oh, Lord, you're stunning," she said, reaching for her messy bun on top of her head, trying to straighten it up before whipping at some crumbs at the corner of her mouth. "I must look like a total mess."

I shook my head. "Course you don't, you're glowing."

"That's because I'm sweating all the time."

Dom let out a little chuckle. "Okay, I'll leave you girls to it. I'll take your bags upstairs."

I nodded. "Oh no, wait, just leave me the carry-on. I've got something in it."

Cassie's face lit up as Dom looked at her with both good humor and tenderness in his face. It was quite intriguing, in fact, as he could switch from the detached man I'd met to the loving man standing in front of me. He had a lot of walls, that man.

Dom sighed and shook his head. "What did you convince her to smuggle for you?"

I frowned. "Was I not supposed to?"

Cassie glared at Dom, rubbing her stomach. "Don't listen to him; he's being dramatic."

Dom turned to me, his eyes still full of mirth. "What?"

"Timbits, maple syrup chocolates, Nanaimo bars..."

Dom laughed a full belly laugh and for a second I was just in awe. This austere man was... beautiful. "Wait until Luca hears about it."

Cassie pointed an accusing finger at him. "You wouldn't dare!"

He leaned down and kissed her forehead. "Your secret is safe with me, munchkin."

"I'm sorry, I didn't know."

Dom rolled his eyes. "Don't worry, she got me to smuggle her food three times this week."

"Four," Cassie replied with a little cheeky smile. "It's just Luca's on my ass about eating healthier for the babies and I do but—" She shrugged.

"He might not be wrong now, is he?" I couldn't help but ask.

"Not you too!" Cassie sighed with exasperation.

Dom raised his hands in surrender. "I'm out of here. I'll leave your suitcase in front of your room." He turned to me, his smile a little more generic than before. "It was nice meeting you."

I nodded, looking at him jog up the stairs with my super heavy suitcase like it weighed nothing at all. That man was something.

When I turned toward Cassie, she was looking at me with a little smile on her face. What was that for?

"Let's go to the kitchen. We can have a cup of tea and chat for a while."

I gave her a side-look. "You want to eat some of the food I brought you, right?"

She laughed. It was so melodious and happy that it eased the remainder of worry I had about her. She was clearly happy. I didn't need to be a psychologist to see that she transpired happiness.

27

"Let me help you; that's why I'm here." I pointed at a chair. "Just sit and tell me where everything is."

I saw she was about to argue when I reached into my bag for the box of Timbits. "Here."

Her face lit up and she took a seat as she grabbed the box from me. "The teapot is in the first cabinet. You can pick the loose herbal teas from the counter just beside the kettle."

I nodded and started to make us tea.

"I'm happy you're here," she said, her mouth full of Timbits.

I couldn't help but laugh because even if I brought her the fifty box; I was not sure I'd see one.

"Where's Jude?"

She sighed. "Boarding school." She shook her head. "I didn't want him to go but Luca said I had to let him do what he wanted. This is a school upstate for little geniuses like him." I shrugged. "He went for their summer program and fell in love with the school." She popped another Timbit in her mouth. "What choice did I have?"

It was a bummer, but I got it. "Luca was right here. Jude's a smart kid; he needs to make his own choices."

She leaned back on her chair. "I know." She rubbed her stomach. "I hope these two will stay with me."

"Yeah…" I was not about to discourage her before her babies were even born.

"My back is really hurting me today so I won't be able to give you a tour of the house."

I shook my head. "Hey, don't worry about it, I don't need a tour. I'll explore as we go." I brought the tray with the tea and cups to the table before sitting across from her.

"I'll have Dom give you a tour later," she added decisively. I'd forgotten how stubborn she could be.

"Dom…" I trailed off. "He's something, isn't he?" I was not sure how to put it; that man was just so hard to read.

She nodded with a small smile. "That's a way to put it, but honestly Dom is the best but don't tell Luca; he might get jealous."

I laughed. "With the way you talk about him? Not a chance, the man is clearly the love of your life."

"That's good to hear."

I looked up, startled at the deep masculine voice coming from the side.

I tried my best to keep my surprise in check at seeing Cassie's husband leaning against the kitchen's threshold, his hand buried in his suit's pants pocket.

His appearance was striking to say the least. He was a tall, wide man, with scars that made him look dangerous and somehow, despite the friendliness of his smile, I suspected he was just as dangerous as he looked.

"Wife," he said commandingly but the softness of

29

his eyes and her blush showed the obvious game between these two.

"It's not what you think," she replied, holding a Timbit between her thumb and forefinger.

"Uh-huh." He walked toward her with a grace I didn't expect, keeping his eyes on her before leaning down slowly and wrapping his mouth around her fingers to steal the Timbit from her.

It was nothing overly special and yet it looked so intimate, so erotic, I felt as if I was intruding.

"Thief..." she breathed, flushed as he let go of her now empty fingers.

He straightened up and gave me a playful wink as he chewed on the sugary goodness.

"It's nice to finally meet you in person, India," he said, standing behind Cassie, wrapping a protective, possessive hand on the side of her neck as she leaned her head against him.

I didn't think they realized it themselves, but they were clearly connected, fitting in to each other in ways we wanted but rarely got.

"You too, Luca. Your house is beautiful. Thank you for inviting me."

He chuckled, rubbing his thumb up and down the back of her neck. "Don't thank me. I'm pleased you could come. It will ease my mind the days I have to go to the city to know you're here with this food smuggler."

"Technically I'm not the smuggler," she said,

laughing and looking up to meet his eyes. "Plus, you did that to me." She pointed to her belly with fake indignation.

"I don't remember you complaining about making them."

"No… but the extra eating is on you."

He cocked his head to the side, pretending to ponder this for a minute. "That's utter shit but A plus for originality. Good attempt."

"Thank you!" She beamed, still looking up at him.

He leaned down and pecked her lips before concentrating on me again. "I'll see you for dinner and try to rein her in tomorrow while Dom and I are away."

Cassie rolled her eyes, but I could see the genuine concern in his eyes.

"Will do!" I promised, having no idea how to rein in this cute little woman who apparently had the power to bend everyone to her will.

He looked at his watch and sighed. "I've got a call in a bit. Be good, okay?" he asked Cassie.

"Always."

He shook his head with a small smile before leaving the room again.

"He is very…" Protective? Powerful? Charismatic? Overwhelming? I was not even sure of what to say.

Cassie smiled, brushing her fingers against her lips as if she could still feel his kiss. "Yeah, he is. Men like him are a different breed."

"Men like what?"

She seemed to be taken aback by my question. "I-What? No, I mean Italian men."

I cocked my head to the side; she seemed too taken aback, too dismissive. There was more to her statement and I made myself a promise to discover what.

D O M

Saying the woman was beautiful was an insult to her. She was breathtaking, the kind of woman to bring you to your knees with just a smile. She was the kind of woman that could bring down an empire... She had Cassie's green eyes but against her caramel skin it looked almost surreal.

She could easily be on the cover of the magazines without using Photoshop, and I hated that she seemed nice and all-seeing as well.

I shook my head. I was happy Luca and I would be gone today, because it felt like when she was around I was mesmerized—just sitting beside her at dinner last night, hearing her melodious voice, smelling her subtle flowery perfume had been torture.

I reached for my suit jacket. As I put it on and put my hand in my pocket, I remembered the piece of paper I'd stuffed in there at the airport.

I got it out and read it again. One word. One stupid, hateful word that could ruin all the hard work I did, ruin the person I became.

'Rapist.' That was a word I hated, a word that woke up the voices haunting me. The voices that I had now managed to quiet most of the time were back, screaming.

I'd looked around, but there was no one in sight. If it had not been for the woman with me, I would have gone to the security office to check the feeds. I couldn't ask for help on this. Luca would go out all guns blazing, and he had enough to worry about these days.

He had to fix all his uncle's stupid decisions, and Lord knew he made a lot of those in his two years of power. He also had to deal with Cassie and the pregnancy that terrified him. I couldn't burden him with that, especially without knowing if it was really something worth his time.

I threw the paper in the trash and rushed downstairs, just to see Luca whispering in Cassie's ear while lovingly cradling her stomach, and India, leaning against the wall, looking at them with a little smile.

My heart tightened in my chest as Cassie looked up at Luca, her eyes full of love and trust. Despite everything she knew, everything he was, she was looking at him like her hero, her knight in his shiny armor.

I was not jealous of them. They deserved nothing more than the happiness they were giving each other, but even if I knew I could never have what they had, I couldn't help this little part of me that envied them, that yearned for this love without conditions, without secrets.

I felt my neck prickle and turned to the side to meet India's inquisitive green eyes; what had she noticed? I couldn't let my guard slip in front of someone like her.

I schooled my face in cold indifference as I held her eyes challengingly.

She kept up with me for a couple of seconds before looking away with a half smile on her lips. She surrendered and yet why did I feel like I'd just lost?

"Ready?" I asked Luca as I descended the last couple of steps.

"Sure." Luca ran his hand down Cassie's cheek. "Be good, okay?"

She grabbed his hand and kissed his palm. "I promise."

I snorted. "Do you know the meaning of being good?"

She glared at me. "You better stop or I won't name my son after you!"

I raised my hands in surrender. God, I loved that woman and when she had told me that their son's middle name would be Domenico in my honor, I had a hard time containing my tears.

"Call me for anything, *si?*" Luca tapped his jacket pocket.

"Of course! Now go and do your thing; we'll be here when you come back."

Luca looked at her for a second, clearly conflicted.

I nudged him forward. "Come on, the sooner we go, the sooner we'll be back."

I leaned down and kissed Cassie's forehead before turning toward India and giving her a cordial nod. I couldn't and shouldn't be outright hostile to her. I knew consciously that she'd done nothing wrong. It was not her fault if she looked like all my wet dreams built into one woman.

Once we settled in the back of the car, and the driver started to pull away, Luca threw a last longing look at the house.

"She'll be fine, Luca. It's only one day."

"I don't like going far these days," he admitted.

"You never like leaving her, since New York and Savio... Not that I blame you, but things are different now. The security is airtight, and she has India with her."

He sighed with a nod. "But you don't like her, do you?"

It was my turn to sigh. Yep, I'd walked right into that one. "It's not that I don't like her. I'm not keen on new people, that's all. She seems nice enough."

"She is lovely, and she seems to genuinely care for Cassie so she's a winner in my book. Plus, let's be honest, she is stunning."

I raised an eyebrow. "Should we tell your wife that?"

He laughed. "She knows. We discussed it last night. I'm happily married, Dom, but I'm neither blind nor dead. Saying anything else would be foolish and a lie which my wife is not fond of."

I shrugged, not really ready to commit to anything.

"I'm just not sure why you dislike her that much. Is it because of the effect she may have on you?"

I snorted. "I'm not discussing this."

"How the tables have turned." Luca grinned at me.

I glared at him, making him laugh. "You were right, it *is* fun." He added, his grin growing wider.

I'd somehow forgotten that Karma was a bitch. "She seems nice enough," I conceded. "It's just weird how someone can just drop their own life like that on a call."

Luca looked away and I knew I touched on something there, but I knew better than to press. Luca would just close off even more.

He sighed. "I just don't see why Matteo needs me to go to that stupid meeting."

"You're the capo, Luca; it's a capi meeting." I shook my head. "I'll deny it until the day I die, but Genovese has been quite good to you, I think. He didn't make many demands."

Luca threw me a surprised look. "I thought I'd never see a day when you agreed with Genovese."

"I know." I faked a shudder. "I am traumatized too."

"I hope it won't last long."

I shook my head. "It shouldn't. Most of what's going on is just between us, but if you want, just leave when you're not needed anymore. I'll take it from there."

Luca exhaled loudly, visibly relieved. "I know it sound—"

"No, it doesn't. It's Cassie." It was enough to say, I knew how much Luca loved her, and I knew how much she loved him. I was also amazed how she could disregard so much in the name of their love and how much happier and more alive he was because of this love. He had nothing more to explain.

Matteo lived in a compound just before entering the city. To be honest, it looked a lot more like a military facility than a home—cold, lifeless, overly organized. Very Matteo actually.

There was the main house in the back where only a few were authorized which Luca and I were privileged… or rather cursed to. The outer building, closer to the main entrance, was the main part of the compound, where the meetings were taking place.

Our car stopped by the security post, and Luca slid down the tinted window to reveal ourselves to the guard.

"Mr. Genovese is expecting you at the house," he said with a nod.

I rolled my eyes. "What the flying fuck does he want now?"

Luca sighed, running a weary hand over his face. "Not sure but it can't be long." He pointed at the couple black sedan already parked by the compound. "Others are already here."

"Oh yeah, like it ever bothered Genovese to make people wait for him."

Matteo Genovese, the capo dei capi—our boss, our king… Our self-appointed God ruled over all of us with an iron fist and inspired so much respect and fear despite only being in his mid-thirties.

He had his favorites—that much was clear—and Luca, luckily or not, was one of them, but it didn't have to mean much with Matteo. Rules were rules; disrespecting him was a death warrant.

"Let's get this over with," Luca muttered, getting out of the car and adjusting his jacket. He glanced at his phone before putting it in the inside pocket of his suit jacket.

We knocked at the door and were let in by a security guy who gestured us toward Matteo's office.

We entered the waiting room just in time to see a tall blond man leaving Matteo's office. Russian... that much was sure.

Luca glared at the man, as I looked down at Enzo, Luca's younger cousin, sitting behind a desk in the waiting room.

Matteo had given him a job as his assistant—not something he really needed or something that Enzo was qualified for really, but it was a way to keep him close, making sure he would not spill the beans on who killed his father and his brother because contrary to what was said within the famiglia, it was not the Albanians who killed the traitors. No, it was Matteo and me. Me because they had taken Cassie and that was worthy of death. Why did Matteo do it? I wasn't sure but the reason had to be selfish; Matteo didn't have a selfless bone in his body.

However, I knew that job was not necessary. Enzo didn't say as much but I knew he had loathed his father and his brother. They were always the first to bully and humiliate him. He would have probably paid us to do that.

"L-L-Luca, how are you?" Enzo asked.

Luca grunted, keeping his eyes on the Russian after he'd passed him and exited the room.

I rolled my eyes. Luca would always be a savage.

"Enzo, you look well." And it was true. It looked

like the kid had more color now, and he was not as painfully thin as he had been a year ago. Being freed of his poisonous home environment did do wonders for him.

Enzo smiled tentatively at me. "T-thank you, Dom. I'm happy," he added, and I couldn't help but notice that even his stutter lessened.

I looked at Luca who was still ignoring us, looking at the door the Russian had taken, a speculative look on his face.

I nudged him before turning to Enzo again. "Matteo asked us to come before the meeting."

Enzo nodded. "Y-you c-can go right in." He gestured to the door.

I elbowed Luca in the kidney, making him grunt.

He turned toward me, a dark glare on his face. "What the fuck did you do that for?"

I gestured to the door. "Move."

I knocked once.

"Come in."

"Was that Alexei Volkov I saw leave your office just now?" Luca asked as soon as I closed the door behind him.

Gianluca Montanari... Smoothness personified.

"Welcome." Matteo gave Luca a small smile. "You know it was."

"The capo dei capi colluding with the Russians? It's bound to make people talk."

Matteo's smile turned into a predatory grin as he

41

reached for his zippo on his black desk and started to play with it. "I was collecting a favor. You know how much I enjoy collecting them, don't you, Gianluca?"

Luca's nostrils flared, and I knew Luca owed him something. I suspected it was to ensure his help in rescuing Cassie from Benny and Savio. I was just scared to find out what Luca had promised him in his moment of weakness.

Matteo sighed, gesturing us to the seats across his desk. Everything in this office was black and glass, cold and emotionless—a true mirror to its owner.

Matteo reached for his cigarettes on his desk and lit one. "I heard you picked up a new stray?"

Luca arched his eyebrows. "How? She arrived yesterday."

Matteo shrugged with a little teasing smile. "I heard she is absolutely stunning. Maybe I should ask her out for dinner."

My stomach dipped down. I felt a burning jealousy even if I had no right or reason to.

Luca shook his head to the side. "Absolutely not."

Matteo leaned back on his seat, arching an eyebrow. "Oh, I see you want that one too? Aren't you greedy? Is your wife happy to share you?"

Luca snorted. "Of course not! I'm monogamous and Cassie is all I need. But India's family and I would not even unleash you on my worst enemy, so on my family?" He winced. "Nope."

I wanted to kiss Luca right there, again I was not

sure why. I wanted to protect India, for Cassie's sake, but I knew I had no right to do it. Luca did though. As the head of the family, he could stick a 'No Touching' sign on her without any speculation.

Matteo laughed. "Fair enough, Montanari. If only you knew the irony of your statement."

I frowned. Matteo seemed to give up way too easily—almost as if he never had any intention to ask India out. That was the most annoying thing about Matteo Genovese... Well, at least *one* of the most annoying things—the man was *always* playing games, always testing, always assessing. You were never sure about what came out of his mouth.

Luca sported a matching frown. "What do you mean?"

Matteo waved his hand dismissively, blowing his smoke toward me. "I'm just messing with you."

"Aren't you always?" I grumbled.

His calm icy-blue eyes turned to me. "Of course I am; that's half the fun," he replied with a teasing smile.

"Why did you want to see us before the meeting?" Luca asked. I guessed he didn't have time for Matteo's antics today—good on him.

"It's about our little issue," he announced, crushing his cigarette in the ashtray.

'Little issue.' That was a way to put it. A traitor was in our ranks, someone smart enough to play Benny and Savio as a puppeteer and get away with it.

That was not a little issue; that was a nuclear bomb, and I wouldn't want to be him once Matteo got his hands on him. Matteo had kept a man alive for five days, torturing him just enough for him to stay alive and suffer before putting an end to him. He looked like calm personified, but he was the most sadistic and demented of us all. A man without a heart, without a conscience, only living by the rules of the famiglia, ready to sacrifice everyone and everything to obtain what he wanted.

"I've got a few leads. Alexei said we should go to Verdi tonight. There's a couple of men we can collect from the side alley when we're ready. We will have a little chat."

'A little chat' for Matteo meant nothing less than a heavy torture session in this building's basement which will end with the guys spilling it all and dying quickly or the guys saying nothing and dying slowly.

Actually, thinking about it, every 'little' thing coming out of Matteo's mouth was an atrocity in the making.

Luca shook his head. "I told you before, I'm not spending a night away from my wife, especially so far along her pregnancy. That's not negotiable."

"But you have that," Matteo waved his hand dismissively, "doctor or whatever living there."

Luca sighed. "She's a psychologist, hardly a doctor, and she could be an obstetric surgeon for all I care. I'm not spending a night away from my wife."

"Young love," Matteo sneered mockingly.

"Something you clearly can't understand," I couldn't help but remind him.

Matteo turned toward me, his eyes full of amusement. "And you can? Actually, maybe the live-in psychologist will give you intensive therapy. We all know you need it."

That reminded me of the note I received, something I really needed to discuss with him.

"*Basta,*" Luca growled, always so defensive of me and our little circle. "Let's start that council meeting now. We didn't come to chitchat."

"Awww, now you're hurting my feelings, Gianluca." He rested his hand on his chest with a pretend pout. "Here I was, sitting, thinking what a delight it was to spend time with the two of you..."

I leaned back on my chair "What would Italians be doing at Verdi? It's Russian territory. It would be stirring up shit. That would be like tattooing yourself as a traitor."

Matteo shook his head. "None of us are that stupid."

"I'm not coming," Luca insisted more forcefully.

Matteo glowered. The man didn't take no for an answer very kindly.

"I'll go," I offered. Luca was my best friend; we had each other's backs. I knew he would have done just the same if the roles were reversed.

Matteo sighed. "I guess I'll just have to make due

with the Wish.com cheap knockoff version of the capo."

I smiled at him. "Take it or leave it." I tried to sound unbothered, but it cut deep because it was how I felt every time we stepped out of the house to do anything with the famiglia.

I already knew how out of place I would feel today when I stepped into the meeting beside Luca, knowing I'd get the speculative looks and Luca would get the looks too. Choosing a simple made man as your consigliere was never done, and yet he'd done it—well, at the same time a capo was not supposed to marry outside the famiglia, and he did that too when he chose Cassie.

Luca was a capo who followed his head and heart more than the old-fashioned rules, and he was just powerful enough to get away with it.

Some were impressed; some were jealous, and some were waiting for him to fall, but I knew better. Luca was the best capo there was.

Matteo jerked his head toward the office door. "You better go ahead. We wouldn't want the others to think you two are the teacher's pets."

Luca sighed but nodded. "The sooner we start, the sooner I'll go home."

"What do you think the Russian had to do in all this?" I asked Luca as soon as we exited the house.

Luca sighed. "Let's walk," he said before gesturing to the driver and telling him in Italian to go park the car in front of the compound by the gate.

Luca buried his hands in his pockets as we took the path to the compound. "I don't know, but Matteo is probably the smartest, most calculating man I've ever met. He won't do anything without having thought of every single possible consequence or outcome."

I threw him a side-look. "You sound both impressed and a little bit in love," I teased.

Luca snorted. "Hardly, but when Matteo is on your side, it's the most lethal weapon at your disposal."

"Do you think he's really on our side?" I couldn't help but ask. As Luca had implied, Matteo was a master manipulator; who was to say he was really working with us? He must have had his own agenda.

"I'll deny it if you ever said anything, but yes, I do." Luca shrugged as the compound came into view. "I know the man would be honest enough to tell us to get fucked if he didn't want to help. I think he needs to figure out if there's a rat in our ranks even more than we do, so yes, as long as our interests are aligned, I think we can trust him."

That was not the best vote of confidence because you could then ask yourself what would happen when your interests and his were not aligned anymore.

I didn't get a chance to even ask more as Romero,

one of the older members of the council, spotted us and told the other bosses who were smoking by the door.

"Let the show begin," I muttered to Luca as we both plastered our cold smiles on our faces.

4

DOM

The meeting was as long and tedious as usual. The bosses had to give their two cents on what the other bosses were doing, and I could see that Luca was getting restless and increasingly annoyed by the questioning of his decisions and his desire to go home. I had to admit this version of Luca was the best yet, a version I never knew he could be, but I guessed that was what the love of a good woman could do to you.

Once the meeting was done, Matteo dismissed the other bosses rather quickly, offering them all free food at his restaurant in town before each of them had their flight homes in their various jets.

"Are you sure you're okay to stay?" Luca asked me one more time before stepping into his car.

I turned around to see Matteo leaning against the door of the compound with a smirk on his face.

I sighed. "Yes, it won't be the first time we've spent quality time together." I had done it after Matteo and I had killed Benny and Savio for kidnapping Cassie and organizing the death of Luca's family. "Just—" I stopped.

"Just?" Luca encouraged, leaning against the door of the car. "Anything."

"I may have promised something to someone and —" I gave him a sheepish smile.

Luca grunted. "What does she want?"

"Donuts from the Donuts Palace... Six." I extended him the paper I had folded in my pocket. "These are the flavors she wants and potential alternatives."

He rolled his eyes, taking the piece of paper from me. "I swear my wife has you wrapped around her little finger."

I couldn't help but smile brightly at that one. "Pot meet kettle."

He chuckled. "That's fair. I'll go get her the food. See you tomorrow, *fratello*."

I walked back toward Matteo once Luca was in the car.

"You two are adorable."

"Uh-huh. It's called friendship; you should try it one day."

"Friendship?" He scrunched his nose in disgust. "That sounds dreadful."

I shook my head. I couldn't help but smile at Matteo's barely veiled disgust.

"What do you want?" Matteo asked as soon as Luca's car disappeared from view.

"What do you mean?"

Matteo rolled his eyes before reaching up for his tie, straightening it. "You jumped way too fast on the opportunity to stay here with me, and I know you don't particularly enjoy my company... despite the fact that I'm an absolute delight."

"You're a sociopath."

"So?" He shrugged. "Both are not mutually exclusive."

"They are."

"Agree to disagree."

"So what do we do now?"

He shrugged. "The meeting ran longer than expected. Let's take the car and go to the city now, then you tell me what you want. Hopefully you won't bore me too much."

"Eager to collect your prize?" I asked, thinking about the poor bastard who was about to cross Matteo's path.

"I'm bored these days. I'll enjoy someone to play with."

"And then you're going to say you're not a sociopath."

"I never said I wasn't."

That shut me up. It was true. Matteo never said he wasn't a sociopath. I remained silent until we reached the interstate, not even sure how I could approach my problem with him—and was it even a problem? It was just a note once...

I sighed as I leaned back on my seat.

Matteo eyed me curiously as he said, "Color me intrigued now. What's gotten your panties in a bunch?"

"Maybe nothing."

"I see." He nodded, switching the gears of his BMW M3. As a true Italian man, he considered automatic transmissions an insult to cars. "I'm losing interest very fast."

I shook my head. "It's just... Who knows about me?"

Matteo's hands tightened on the steering wheel before giving me a wary look. That was not a look I was used to coming from Matteo Genovese... He was not the wary type.

"Cosa vuol dire?"

I frowned. Matteo rarely reverted to Italian despite being a native speaker. "What I mean is who knows about my upbringing, what my father was. What he—" I winced as I swallowed past the ball of shame in my throat. "Made me do."

His grip on the steering wheel loosened as his shoulders relaxed. "Ah." Did he just seem relieved? Why would he be? "Not many people anymore. Romero, Luca, me..." He shook his head. "Your father's side *business* was not something most of us were proud of."

"And yet, nobody did anything."

He shrugged. "It was not my place. Nobody asked me to intervene, and he was bringing a lot of money to the famiglia. Money has a tendency to make you go blind."

I shook my head. Go say that to the thirteen-year-old boy I'd once been. Go say that to all the young girls my father stole and destroyed. Go say that to my mother who had chosen to take her own life when I was merely a boy instead of being raped once more by the evil scum that shared my DNA.

But no matter what I couldn't hold that against Matteo because despite what he'd thought, he had only been fifteen himself at the time. He was seeing himself as a man, but he was what I'd been... just a boy.

"Why are you asking?"

I sighed. "I don't know. I just wonder."

"You just wonder?" He nodded. "Uh... *Quanto pensi che sia stupido?*"

I rolled my eyes. "I don't think you're stupid. I was just wondering, truly."

"*Bene*. Have it your way," he replied, parking in a darkening street in front of the alley behind Verdi.

I looked at my watch. "How long do we need to stay here?"

Matteo leaned back on his seat, sitting more comfortably. "Why? Am I boring you already?"

I threw him a side-look. We both knew that we didn't really enjoy each other's company that much.

"Shouldn't be too long. He said he's supposed to come to work around this time. He'll text me when we're ready to collect."

I turned fully toward Matteo now. It was not just a random guy that the Russians would be giving us; it was one of their own.

"What did Volkov want from you?" I crossed my arms on my chest. "It has to be something important for him to give you one of his own."

Matteo shrugged. "It's not really one of their guys. It's an opportunistic Albanian who seemed to be feeding at every table and when did we become *confidanti,* you and I?"

"I'm not saying I'm your confidant, Genovese." I shrugged. "We're going to be sitting in this car for God knows how long. Do you just want to do it in total silence?" Actually, maybe it was for the best. I sighed. "Just forget about it."

Matteo kept his eyes on the alleyway for a couple more minutes before talking. "He wanted the only thing that makes men like him weak. Love."

I turned toward him, remaining silent. I did agree that love could make you weaker but not the right kind of love, not the real one. True love, the one Luca and Cassie shared, made you so much stronger. It could make you climb even the highest most arduous obstacle and that was beautiful.

"So what's the secret? Just don't love?" I asked mockingly.

"No," Matteo replied, his voice somehow lower, darker. "The secret is not not to love; you can't stop the virus once it's in. The secret is to remove every potential risk from your life."

"This is quite a lonely existence."

Matteo let out a tired laugh. "*Lo so.*"

He knew? How did he know? Had the cruel king, the coldest man I'd ever met, once been at a risk of thawing?

"Are you telling me—"

"Here." Matteo pointed at the alleyway and the unconscious man that had been thrown out by two big guys with Russian Mafia tattoos on their necks.

I was somehow grateful for the interruption. I was about to ask the stupidest question. There was no chance of Matteo Genovese ever being at risk of falling in love. Men like him didn't feel anything other than contempt, anger and a touch of sadism. I did feel sorry for the poor woman who would eventually have to marry him and give him an heir.

"Go pick him up; we don't have all night."

I pointed at my chest. "Why me?" I shook my head. "You wanted him."

Matteo arched an eyebrow. "Are you questioning *my* orders? *My* orders? Are you forgetting who I am?"

How could I forget? And yes, questioning his orders was beyond stupid and yet, I couldn't help but hold his eyes, just a few seconds longer. Maybe I did have a death wish after all.

"You pick him up; I play with him." He gestured to the unconscious man by the overflowing dumpsters. "Unless," His smile turned predatory. "I go pick him up and you play. Is that what you want, Domenico?"

I remained stoic but I cringed inwardly. I'd seen Matteo *'play'* a couple of times and it was something I never would have been able to do.

I sighed, opening the car door. "Pop the trunk open."

Matteo snorted. "That's what I thought."

I walked down the alley and nodded my head to the two Russians waiting by the door to ensure successful pickup of the package.

I turned the guy over; there was no mark on him. I looked up, throwing a questioning look at the Russians.

The shorter one reached in his pocket to show me an empty syringe. "Work smart, not hard," he said with his heavy accent; this one was from Mother Russia.

I pulled the guy up and huffed. Fuck, he was heavier than he looked.

"A little help?"

The biggest one reached for his cigarettes. "Not our job, *mudak*. We delivered you the package. It's your problem now. Boss said to make sure we can't find him."

"That won't be a problem, *coglione*." He called me shithead in Russian; I was just returning the favor. "After the boss is done with him? Nobody would ever recognize him."

I struggled to take him to the car, and Matteo decided to be a prime asshole and didn't even come help me lift him in the trunk despite all my huffing and puffing.

The trunk itself was lined with black washable plastic and I was wondering how many body parts this trunk had carried to make plastic a permanent feature.

"Thanks for helping me," I spat breathlessly when I joined him in the car.

"Oh, you needed help?" he asked me, starting the car and driving a little faster than I would have liked. I guessed the man was more excited to play with his prey than I anticipated.

"What do you think?" I asked, readjusting my clothes before putting some order in my hair.

"I think that the big, strong and brave Domenico Romero never needs anyone."

The sarcasm was strong with that one... Asshole!

———

I took a sip of the drink Matteo served me as I waited for the Albanian to wake up.

Matteo had tied him to a chair in the middle of the room over an hour ago, and both of us were getting a little impatient now.

I leaned back on my chair and looked around Matteo's playroom. Well, that was what he called his basement—the playroom. It had nothing to do with that *Fifty Shades of Grey* crap. No, it was far from being that type of playroom.

I looked at all the instruments he had on the far wall. This basement was nothing more than a torture room.

Matteo sighed, looking at the clock on the wall. "Seriously, what the fuck did they give him?" He growled with frustration. "Do you think he'll wake up if I cut his pinky?" he asked, reaching for the pruning shears on the metal table.

Everything in this basement was made of metal and concrete. My eyes drifted to one of the drains on the floor, just under the Albanian. The drains that became useful when the room was hosed down to make all the blood disappear after one of Matteo's 'discussions.'

That was the moment the Albanian grunted and lifted his head, blinking rapidly.

"It's like he heard you," I teased Matteo before taking another sip of my drink.

"I know." He cocked his head to the side, putting the shears back on the table. "If only he had waited a minute longer; I was really looking forward to it."

I knew that was not a joke either; he was a true sadist.

The guy's eyes widened when he finally came back to full consciousness and started to spat things in Albanian. I didn't need to speak the language to know that none of his words were friendly.

Matteo seemed completely unfazed by the outburst as he removed his suit jacket and put it on the back of the chair he had been previously occupying.

He concentrated on the man who was still shouting in Albanian. His face was red, the veins of his neck almost popping as he glared at us, the hate behind his eyes, unmissable.

He moved his arms, trying to remove his restraint, then screamed in pain as the metal cut into his flesh.

That binding was one of Matteo's pride and joys —rope mixed with barbed wire. The more you struggled, the more it gripped you.

Matteo stood in front of him stoically, his light-blue eyes just as cool and expressionless as the ice man he was.

"Are you done?" he asked with a calm, even tone once the man stopped screaming. "I won't lie to you; you're going to die tonight. There's no question about it, but you can choose how you die. If you speak now, I'll give you a quick and painless death," he said, tapping his holster holding his gun. "Or we can make a game of it." He gestured to his basement wall, which proudly held most of his torture equipment. "I've got enough fluid and skills to keep you alive at least two days in excruciating pain. Personally, I'd like for you to pick option two. I finished my show on Netflix and I'm a little bored."

"What show?" I couldn't help but ask.

"Sociopath Unchained."

"Ah." I nodded. "Isn't that the masterclass you taught?"

Matteo's lips lifted slightly on the corner; it was the closest the man ever came to a genuine smile. "It was indeed." He turned to the guy who was looking at Matteo with burning hate in his eyes. "So, what will it be?"

"Fuck off, Italian filth. I'm not telling you shit!"

Matteo's face broke into a wide grin, like a kid on Christmas morning. "Good answer!" He turned toward me. "Do you want to stay and watch me play?"

I shook my head with a low chuckle. "No, thanks.

I think I'll go upstairs and have some of the amazing lasagna your housekeeper made."

He shrugged. *"Fai come vuoi.* I'll see you in a while; just help yourself."

I threw the Albanian another look, almost feeling bad for him. He had no clue what was about to be unleashed on him.

I called Luca as soon as I closed the basement door behind me and gave him a quick rundown of the situation.

I grabbed a container of lasagna, and I'd just put it in the oven when Matteo walked into the kitchen with a sigh.

I looked at him as he wiped his wet hands on a red towel. I suspect it was a color picked on purpose.

"Already?" I looked down at my watch. "It's only been twenty minutes."

"I know." He shook his head. "It's always the ones who think they are tough who crack first. I just put like what? Two razor blades under his nails and he was singing like a nightingale."

"A canary?"

"What?" Matteo frowned, throwing the towel on his shoulder. *"Cantava come un usignolo."*

I nodded. "I know in Italian it's nightingale, but in English it is canary."

"Perche?"

"Perche no?" I replied. I had no fucking clue why; it was just the way it was.

He rolled his eyes, waving his hand in a dismissive gesture. "Thank you for the English lesson of 'nobody fucking cares.' I'll teach you how to torture one day."

"Did you find out anything?" I asked as I knew better than to antagonize him further. I let my eyes trail down and stopped at his collar. "You've got some blood there." I touch the corner of my own collar.

"He was a bleeder," he confirmed with a nod.

"So, Did you find out anything?"

He twisted his mouth to the side, clearly not overly happy. "Either Volkov is playing me, or this man was pretending to know more than he did." He walked to the fridge and grabbed a bottle of water. He took a long sip. "He said the man they spoke with sounded young and from New York."

"I see... That narrows it down."

He rolled his eyes. "At least it was what I expected —it wasn't Benny or Savio. He said the man called himself *Mano Vendicativa.*"

"The vengeful hand?"

We both grimaced; that was beyond cheesy.

"He never met the man. He was careful and only spoke with different burner phones. He said he had a plan that the famiglia would fall, and when he'll be on top, he'll remember."

"Um, so we don't have much?"

He shook his head sharply. "No, but apparently

there's a guy named Hoxha—also known as the 'living ghost.'"

"Do you know who he is?"

"Not yet but it's only a matter of time, and when I do…" His nostrils flared, the only physical sign of his irritation. "Nothing will be able to save him."

"I have no doubt." And it was true. Matteo was like a hunting dog. Once he was on his trail, I would not want to be this living ghost.

The oven pinged and I jerked my head toward it. "Want some?"

He shook his head. "I'll go shower. You can stay here tonight, it's late. There's a room ready, first floor, second door on the left."

I had not expected his concern—this was not Matteo at all—and despite everything, I couldn't help but ask. "Why?"

"Why what?"

"Why are you helping us with all that?"

He turned around slowly, meeting my eyes. "Having a smart rat in our rank is not good."

"He is not against you."

"He is taking out the famiglia without my authorization. He is against me. He is smart and cunning. I can't have that acting against us."

I looked at him silently for a second. "Is that all there is?"

"What else could it be?" He shrugged. *"Sono l'uomo*

dal cuore di ghiaccio." he added before leaving the room.

I looked down at my lasagna... The man with the heart made of ice... And for the first time since I'd met Matteo Genovese, I was wondering if it was not all pretend.

5

INDIA

I was twenty-seven years old and yet I felt like a teenager about to meet the asshole bully she had a crush on. Except that I was not a teenager, and Domenico was neither my crush nor my bully, and yet I checked on my outfit and hairdo three times before going to look for him in the manor.

I made sure to wear my best pair of jeans, the ones that really made my ass look good and my red top that revealed just enough to entice.

That man was truly a mystery with two so different sides of him. I saw his little attentions toward Cassie, his gentleness and good humor. I heard him speak on the phone with Jude and it had been beyond cute and yet, as soon as I entered the room or appeared in his line of vision, he turned to ice. I could almost see the wall being erected around him, and it rubbed me the wrong way.

It might have been the psychologist in me, but I needed to understand why he was going out of his way with me when it was clearly not in his nature to be cold and dismissive. Did he think I was a threat to his family?

He had to see the truth. I'd been here over a week now and except for the forced conversation we were having during dinner or when forced together, he had not warmed up to me, and I didn't like it.

My phone vibrated on my bed and some of the apprehension I felt at seeking Dom faded. Jake's name flashed on the screen... Why was he calling me? How dared he call me? I could feel my cheek-bone tingle as I rejected his call. I had wanted to block his number, but then who knew what he'd do to contact me? He wouldn't come here; that much I knew, and if he tried, I knew he would face men that would teach him some manners.

Maybe he should come and see how people his own size reacted to his attitude. He looked like everything a woman would want and I had to admit his interest had caused me to falter. He was rich, good-looking, and well mannered—apparently a gift to women... a poisoning gift to say the least.

I sighed, shaking my head. I would not let Jake

Warner steal one more good moment from my life, one more smile or one single second of happiness he didn't deserve it. I arranged my curls so they fell nicely around my shoulders and trying to ignore the excitement that settled in the pit of my stomach at seeing the tall sullen man who seemed to dislike me on principle.

I found him in the game room sitting at the chess table, facing a laptop. He was playing a game with someone I couldn't see.

"Knight in D3? Are you sure, little man?"

"Dom, just move my piece."

I was not really familiar with the voice but based on the youth of the tone it could only be Jude.

Dom chuckled. "So bossy, you do belong in this family."

I studied him. He was talking to Jude with evident pride and affection—a look I'd been seeing a lot on his face... Well, except for me; that was clear.

He was dressed in black dress pants and a white button-up shirt rolled up to his elbows, revealing his tanned, muscled forearms. I'd never considered forearms as attractive, and yet I could barely stop looking at them as he moved the pieces around the board.

I didn't feel comfortable spying on their moment, but I felt compelled to keep on going; that man was a mystery to me.

"How's Cassie?"

"Cassie's doing great, kid. She's so excited for you

to come home and meet the babies. Didn't you talk to her yesterday?"

"I did but she's always trying to shield me. You're not. I know you'll tell me the truth."

Dom looked up and met my eyes through the gap in the door.

"Always," he said with a sure voice, keeping his eyes on me in a way that challenged me from saying otherwise.

He did just lie to the kid though. Cassie wasn't great. She had contractions and that was why she and Luca were gone today, and it was also why I was seeking the man who disliked me.

I heard a loud bell coming from the computer.

"Got to get to class. Thanks for the game. We'll finish it tonight."

Dom looked down at the screen and winked at Jude. "Sure thing, kiddo. Enjoy learning."

"Always!"

He sighed, closing the laptop. "Are you always spying on people?" he asked, staying on his chair, sprawling into it like a king in his kingdom.

I shrugged, trying to sound and look as if I was not embarrassed. "You're not the most forthcoming person. I have to try to figure out who you are," I admitted. There was no shame in that.

"There's no need." He stood up, straightening his back, once more reminding me how broad he was. "Was there anything you needed?"

I nodded. "Yes. Cassie left a little in a panic this morning, and she talked about turning the flowers in the greenhouse. I promised I would, but I'm not sure what she meant."

He looked out the window and the bright sunlight hit his face from an angle showing me that his eyes were actually not as dark as I thought. They were a darker honey than actual brown.

He turned toward me again and gave me a sharp nod. "Don't worry. I'll take care of it." He stood in front of the door, frowning down at me, still blocking his path. "What are you doing?"

I looked up, standing my ground. It was fairly rare that I could actually look up to a man.

"I want to help. That's why I'm here."

He shook his head. "Not necessary. I said I'll do it," he replied—or rather barked back.

I was grating him the wrong way, but I knew it was the best way to get at least a genuine reaction.

He tried to bypass me, but I moved in his way again.

"What?"

"I want to help. Please let me help."

He grunted. "You won't let it go, will you?"

I shook my head. "I'm just as stubborn as Cassie when she wants donuts."

I could see him fighting his smile. "Nonsense. Nobody is that stubborn."

I nudged his arm softly. "Come on, give me a chance. I'm not that bad."

"Fine," he let out on a sigh, looking heavenward. "Let's go."

I followed him silently to the greenhouse and was taken aback by how big and full it was. There were so many colors; it barely looked real.

"It's... wow," I said for lack of better words.

He smiled. "Yes, Cassie has a gift." He pointed at the long, narrow wooden table. "We need to switch the flowers from this table to the shaded area." He pointed to an area covered with a dark-green plastic tarpaulin.

"Why do we need to do that?" I frowned, looking at the little purple flowers in the pots.

He shrugged. "I don't know and I don't ask. I just do what the woman wants me to do. The hormones make her downright scary."

"And horny." I winced at the memory of where Cassie's hands were on Luca yesterday when I walked unannounced in the library... a mistake I would never make again.

"Yeah, I don't think we can entirely blame the hormones for whatever you witnessed. Just be grateful you didn't get here when she was small enough to get freaky. I've seen part of her and him I wished I'd never seen," he added, faking a shiver.

"Lord help us all."

He looked at me with a small smile, and it was nice to be the recipient of one of those.

"You see, I'm not a terrible person," I offered as I picked up one of the flowerpots and started toward the shaded area.

"I never said you were. It's just that I'm not keen for strangers to invade our space. I want to keep the family safe. It's not personal."

"It feels personal." I turned toward him, holding the pot close to my chest. "You know I'm not completely clueless."

He stood straighter, his jaw taut, his fingers tightening around the terracotta pot he was holding. "What do you mean?"

Now was the time to come clean. Maybe it would ease his weariness about me.

I sighed, resting the pot I was holding back on the table.

"As we both know Cassie is quite chatty, and after she announced to me she got married, she actually got quite... quiet about her husband." I shrugged. "I first thought he might be abusive and it scared me," I admitted. "But then I found this amazing thing called Google and it explained a lot."

"Did it?"

I wiggled my fingers in the air. "It was all rumored of course; the word 'alleged' was used a lot, so you know," I cocked my head to the side, causing my fringe to get into my eyes. I huffed it off. "I gave it the benefit of the doubt, and then I came here and it all became clear. The rumors were much more than mere allegations."

He slowly put the potted plant back on the table, keeping his eyes trained on my face. His face was a mask of coldness, but he looked more wary than hostile at that moment.

"What are you going to do about it?" His voice was eerily calm and composed, making it a little terrifying.

"Nothing." I shrugged. "Cassie is extremely happy, so much more than I could have hoped, and Luca is clearly a good man, at least by my standards, and on top of it... I don't want to die."

"Ah," He nodded. "Okay then." He picked up his potted plant again and resumed his walk to the shaded area.

I followed him with my eyes, watching how his back muscles moved under his tight white dress shirt.

"Okay then?" I repeated. That had been such an anticlimactic answer.

He put the plant on the floor and grabbed another one before throwing me a quick look. "What?"

"No, it's just—" I shook my head. "I don't know. It's just not what I expected."

"I swear, you girls really need to stop watching films." He grumbled before pointing to the pot I'd put back on the table. "More working, less talking. You wanted to help; let's move."

I flushed at the embarrassment at being reprimanded like a teenager, but I sucked it up and finished the task in silence. It had been a sort of comfortable silence as if there was a truce between us. The atmosphere, while not peaceful, was obviously not as tense.

"What did you expect?" he asked me thirty minutes later when we exited the greenhouse after completing all the detailed tasks Cassie had left in a little notebook.

"What do you mean?" I asked, walking beside him. If I remembered correctly, it was the first time he actually instigated conversation between us.

"You said you didn't expect my reaction; what did you expect?" He stopped and turned toward me briskly, making me recoil.

HIs frown deepened at his reaction. "I'm not going to hurt you."

"No. I know, it's just—" I stopped and looked down, my cheeks burning with embarrassment. Some things were better kept in the secret box of my head. "I just thought you would be more annoyed at the truth."

He shook his head, resuming his walking. "It is what it is. Loyalty is crucial in this family but I'm sure you know that."

"I do."

"Okay then."

Before I thought better of it, I grabbed his arm just as he reached for the back door. I felt his biceps tense under my fingers. This man was seriously buffed.

He froze and looked at my hand on his arm as if it was hurting him.

"There's more though, isn't there?"

"You're beautiful."

I let go of his arm. Of all the things I expected, this was not it.

I'd heard that a lot, especially since I'd reached puberty, but somehow coming from him, it was different. It pleased me that he thought I was beautiful, but at the same time it sounded much more like a flaw than anything else, coming from his mouth.

"Okay. Should I apologize for that? It's just genetics."

He sighed. "No." He opened the door and jerked his head in as a silent invitation to follow him.

I walked behind him and stayed by the back door, looking at him as he grabbed the bottle of scotch from the top shelf in the kitchen.

"Want one?"

I shook my head. "No, thank you. I don't drink." *Anymore.*

"Okay, I'll have yours," he announced, serving himself an impressively large shot.

"So your problem with me is that I'm beautiful?" I

said, showing him I was not ready to let that one go, and also I enjoyed saying that. I enjoyed the fact that he found me beautiful even if truth be told it had sometimes been more a hindrance in life than anything else.

He threw me an annoyed glare that almost made me smile.

"The problem is not that you're beautiful. The problem is that you're supposed to be this stunning successful psychologist with this amazing life in Canada, and after Cassie phoned you about the pregnancy being a little more difficult than she'd expected, you just up and left." He took a sip of his drink, keeping his eyes on me as if he was looking for any tell, and he probably was. Too bad he was playing with an expert. "You never talk about your life there, never mention friends, boyfriends, anything... I'm sorry to say that sounds suspicious."

I nodded. "Says the guy with one friend."

He raised two fingers. "Two actually. Two and a half if you count the kid." He gave me a small smirk. "Plus, I've got a good excuse for that one. My job's not that great for making friends."

He did have a point. I didn't need to be an expert in Mafia to guess it was quite a solitary world.

I sat on a stool across from him.

"You know you could have asked instead of acting all suspicious. Communication is important in every relationship."

"We *don't* have a relationship."

Ouch that hurt. "We do. There are many different types of relationships, you know—not all of them involve romantic feelings and sex. We have a relationship, even if we are merely more than acquaintances." I shook my head.

His scowl deepened. "I'm not looking for therapy."

I could see I was not going to get anywhere with him. He was too defensive. Maybe later, when he trusted me.

"I'm still working, you know."

He arched his eyebrows as he sipped on his drink, the only sign of his surprise.

"I'm a successful therapist, even if Cassie probably oversold it," I said with a small smile. "I work for an online therapy company called *BZen*. I'm a registered therapist there and all my sessions are via Zoom. It allows me to have a certain flexibility in life I enjoy, and it also allows me to have complete control of my schedule and work location." I shrugged. "It may pay a little less than having your own practice in person, but it's worth it for me." I looked at my watch. "I have three sessions today. I had one this morning and I have one in a couple of hours." I traced the pattern on the white marble breakfast bar with my forefingers. "As for my family, there's only my mother and she's been traveling for a while—well, for the past nine years. She started when I entered university. She's been looking for herself; I hope she finds whatever she is looking for." I cleared my throat. I was getting thirsty now and somehow regretted not saying yes to the glass of scotch. I was not the same girl as I had been, and Dom was not Jake.

He got a peach iced tea pitcher from the fridge and filled a glass before sliding it toward me. I didn't even think he realized it, but it revealed a lot about his character. He was reacting on instinct. No matter what he said, he was of a caring nature.

"You don't seem bitter about having an absentee mother."

"She was not an absentee; she was being her. I can't blame her for trying to find meaning in her life. She raised me well. I always had food on the table, clean clothes, a warm bed... When I turned eighteen and started university, she left." I shrugged. "I had an interesting childhood."

"I'm sure you did."

"I'll tell you all about it one day." I was not sure why I volunteered that information. "What about you?"

"What about me?"

I rolled my eyes. He was such a textbook avoider. "Your childhood."

He shrugged, finishing his glass in one go. He looked away for a second, his eyes clouding with pain.

I was about to ask how he was feeling when his face reverted to his coolness and he shrugged again.

"Oh, you know, the classics—murder, racket, horse races, razor blades under my cap."

"You literally just described an episode of *Peaky Blinders*."

"So what?" He grinned at me. "*Peaky Blinders* is an awesome show."

I chuckled. "You're an idiot."

He cocked his head to the side, a light of amusement in his eyes. He never looked at me like that before and it did things to my stomach I had not felt in a very long time.

"Is that your professional diagnosis?"

No, my professional diagnosis is that someone hurt you beyond repair and that even if you crave love, you don't know how to let anyone love you. "Yes, it is."

He nodded. "You're spot on. I guess you're legit. You don't only have the looks, you have the brain too." His phone vibrated in his pocket. "I'll see you later, Doctor. *Pronto?*"

I looked at him exiting the room. Did he even realize how complimentary he was? Probably not and it made his compliment much more worth it.

———

I felt really good this afternoon. The session I just had with my patient was very productive and I felt useful. This was the main reason why I had decided to become a psychologist. I saw the trauma, the pain, and I wanted to help. I'd wanted to help people get some inner peace.

"India, can I see you for a minute?"

I stopped at the bottom of the stairs, looking at Luca leaning against the threshold of the small library.

Luca was a nice man, but he was not the type to chitchat; that much was clear.

"Um, yeah, sure. Is Cassie okay? I was just about to go make her some tea."

He nodded with a small smile, easing some of my worry. "Yes, she's okay. I was just up there; she is taking a nap. It won't be long." He moved from his spot in front of the door in a silent invitation for me to follow him in.

Once I walked in, he closed the door and gestured me to the brown leather chair across from the fireplace.

"Did I do something wrong?" I asked, worried about myself now. He was a Mafia boss after all.

"No, of course not," he scoffed, sitting across from me. "Thank you for taking care of Cassie the way you do. She can't stop raving about the pressure points that ease her pain or the herbal teas that are doing wonders for her stomach and other little issues."

I shrugged, unsure where he was going with that.

"You're more than welcome. It's no trouble. Cassie is adorable."

He nodded. "She really is," he confirmed, a small tender smile sprouting in the corner of his scarred mouth.

"And the herbal tea is nothing special. My mother trained as a holistic doula; I learned a lot with her."

"Yes." He sighed, looking toward the unused fireplace. "The doctor will perform a C-section on Cassie; she is scheduled in two weeks." He studied me with his keen eyes. "You don't seem surprised."

I shook my head. "I'm not. I suspected that much. Cassie is tiny and she is quite big with still four weeks to go, but you know twins rarely go to term, and a C-section might be the safest for the three of them."

"Yes, so he said, and he knows better than to lie to a capo, am I right?"

My heart sank in my stomach. He knew that I knew. *Fuck you, Dom!*

"This is actually what I wanted to talk to you about." He continued when I remained silent.

"I won't tell anyone. Who would I even tell?"

"No, I know, it's just—" He looked away, gathering his thoughts. "Dom said you knew most of it."

"Well, I know the rumors."

He gave me a side-look. "Let's drop pretenses, shall we? I'm the East Coast Capo of the Italian Mafia."

I tried to keep my face smooth as my mind screamed, *Lord, just walk away; you don't want to hear that. You'll end up dead!* But all I said was "Okay?"

I might not have fooled him as well as I hoped because he quickly continued. "I'm not going to hurt you, and neither will Dom even if I know he has been a little mean to you."

I snorted. "Ah, don't sell him short. He has been a complete ass."

Luca laughed. "That's Dom," he confirmed. "I'll ask him to back down."

I waved my hand dismissively. "I'm used to bullying. Let him give me his best."

Luca frowned. "You don't really look or act like a girl who's been bullied."

"I'm a half-Indian girl—called 'India.' How do you think school went for me?"

He grimaced.

I chuckled. "Exactly! My mother is adorable but scatterbrained and as happy-go-lucky as they come. She's the epitome of the Hippie Boho. She went to a yoga retreat in India when she was twenty. She met that charismatic Indian Yogi, and I was conceived. She called me India because that was where I was conceived."

"I see."

I laughed. Somehow, I didn't think he did. His house, his clothes, his way of speaking, everything

about him screamed traditional, severe upbringing...
Mafia or no Mafia.

"Okay, so going back to the subject of my... line of
work." He continued with an even tone, keeping his
eyes locked on me. I suspected Luca was a bit like me
—gifted at reading people.

'Line of work.' That was a way to put it.

"I'm listening."

"I don't want you to be upset with Cassie."

Okay, that didn't go the way I expected. "I'm not.
Why would I be?"

"She wanted to tell you—about me, us, and the life
we lead—but I discouraged her from doing so."

I nodded. "Because you didn't know if you could
trust me; it makes sense."

He shook his head. "No, well..." He cocked his
head to the side. "Maybe partially but Cassie trusted
you. That was enough credential for me. No, it was
more the fact that knowing the truth has the potential to put you in danger."

I tried to swallow past the lump of anxiety
settling in my throat.

"I'll keep you safe; Dom will keep you safe." He
leaned forward on his chair, resting his forearms on
his thighs. "But the only thing Cassie wanted was
your safety, nothing more."

I leaned forward too and reached over to squeeze
his hand.

"I never doubted her. Cassie is a lot of things but not petty. I understand and I promise to be careful."

He nodded. "Good, I just wanted to clarify."

I knew when I was getting dismissed.

I stood up and started toward the door but stopped before I could stop myself.

"I know you're scared for her and I get it. She's one of the most important people in your life and you've already lost so much. But she is doing good."

He gave me a small smile. "I know she is but this fear—" He tapped the center of his chest with his forefinger. "I can't smother it. I can barely contain it. The irrational part of me just wants to sweep her away and lock her in a tower surrounded by pillows to make sure that no harm will ever come to her, ever. Because while your assessment is quite accurate, it has a major flaw." He took a deep breath. "Cassie is not *one* of the most important people in my life; she *is* my life. She is the person, the one that brought me back to life. She is not just my wife and my love… she is my everything."

I looked at this big, scarred, terrifying man being brave enough to bare his soul and admit out loud the extent of his love for Cassie, and I could not help the tiny pinch of envy that squeezed my heart.

Would I ever be lucky enough to be loved that way? Would I ever be deserving enough?

"Then you're both blessed… in a terrifying sort of way." I smiled at him. "I'll go make her tea now. See you later and thank you for being honest," I added before exiting the room.

Dom was just walking in the back door as I entered the kitchen. I scowled silently in his direction before turning toward the cabinets to prepare the tea.

I expected him to just walk by, like he couldn't see me, like he'd been doing every time we were alone and he didn't have to pretend for Cassie's sake.

It was why I startled when he spoke.

"Why the scowl?" he asked casually.

I turned around, the scowl still very much present on my face.

He reached for a red apple in the fruit bowl, rubbed it on his dress shirt over his pec, and took a big bite, completely unfazed about what I liked to call 'my glare of death.'

"What?" he asked, his mouth still full of apple.

"You ratted me out? Nice."

"So what?"

I crossed my arms on my chest. "Snitches end up in ditches!"

He burst into laughter, the kind of laughter that made you cry, snortle, and caused stomach cramps. He was almost bent in two laughing so hard he was gasping for air.

"God, what's that noise?" Luca asked, walking into the room. His face broke into a wide smile as he took in Dom's face, his eyes shining with his tears of laughter.

"She just threatened me!" He gasped in between his annoying laughs and pointed a finger at me as his laughter subsided a little. "Snitches end up in ditches, she said…" He shook his head. "Snitches end up in ditches!" he repeated, his laughter picking up yet again.

I wished deep down that he would just choke on his laughter. *Asshole*!

Luca turned toward me, trying to look serious, but his eyes were radiating with mirth.

"Well, she's not wrong. Snitches do end up in ditches. But isn't the saying 'Snitches get stitches?'"

"Maybe," I grumbled. *Damn you, Paul Bettany*!

Dom wiped at the tears under his eyes. "In Italian you say, *la spia non è figlio di Maria*." He shook his head, catching his breath. "That's the hardest I laughed in…"

"I don't think I ever heard you laugh that hard before actually." Luca piped up, looking at me with speculation in his eyes.

"From which Mafia movie is that from?" Dom asked, having regretfully recovered without dying. "You're probably sharing your poor cinematic references with Cassie."

I shrugged, turning toward the cabinet again to prepare Cassie's tea. I would die before admitting where I'd heard that one from.

"*Dai, lasciala in pace.* Come with me to the office; I've got to discuss New York."

Dom chuckled with a shake of his head. "Sure, I'll leave her alone. See you later, mobster lady."

They both left me in the kitchen, walking away and laughing together, while I prepared the tea with murder on my mind.

INDIA

I looked at Cassie as she sat on the bed, propped against the bed frame, trying to balance her little red stress ball on her very round stomach.

I sighed, sitting by her feet. "How are you doing? Really?" I asked, reaching over and massaging her swollen ankle gently.

She gave me a little shrug, with a small pout that made me smile. "I'm okay. It's just—" She rubbed at her belly gently. "Jude just came back and I'm too tired and sore to do anything with him, and now I'll uproot him for New York for half of his vacation."

Jude had been just as much a ray of sunshine as I'd imagined him to be, and so freaking smart too. I'd almost forgotten I was speaking with an eleven-year-old boy and seeing him with Luca—the man acted with a pride almost paternal when Jude recounted his many successes at school and how he thrived there.

"You know that this boy is wise beyond his years, right? Plus, I'm sure he'll enjoy spending some time in the city. I'll take him to shows and everything." I squeezed her leg. "He knows how much you love him, and he is clearly excited to meet his nephew and niece soon."

"Yes, I have a hard time believing the babies will be here in a week."

I frowned. She sounded more worried than elated. "Are you not excited?"

"No, yes. I mean—" She sighed, leaning her head back, looking at the ceiling. "I love my babies. How could I not? They are part Luca and part me. I'm so excited to see them, but I'm also scared, you know? I'm going to be a mom, and the world we live in…" She stopped, looking away with shame.

I wanted to tell her that I knew the truth, that it was okay, but I had promised Luca to wait until the babies were born.

"It's true, the world is dangerous, but these babies have you and Luca. A loving, caring mother and a fiercely protective father." I winked at her. "These kids won the golden ticket."

Her shoulders relaxed as she leaned more on the pillows behind her back. "Yes, I guess you're right."

Her tense smile turned genuine, and I knew I had said exactly what I needed to say.

"You know what I'd like though?"

I threw her a side-look. "Let me guess? Sweets?"

Her smile widened, giving her a cute cheeky look. It was hard to identify her with the twenty-two-year-old pregnant Mafia wife she'd become. She barely looked old enough to drive, and the innocence shining out of her made her look even more youthful, even if I knew how fierce and combative she really was.

I chuckled. "I need to go to the store. I'm sure a trip to the local sweet store can be arranged."

"Yes, you can ask Dom to take you."

I winced. I couldn't imagine spending time alone in a car with Dom who had been calling me 'mobster lady' every chance he got.

"Can anyone else take me? Maybe I can go by myself. You've got like five cars here."

She frowned. "Why? Did something happen? Was Dom mean to you?"

I shook my head. Now was not the moment to approach my concerns with Dom and my infuriating attraction to him. "I just don't want to bother him. He's probably super busy now getting everything ready for the trip to New York."

She cocked her head to the side, considering it, and I thought I had won until she spoke again. "Luca doesn't trust many people except for Dom, you know." She twisted her mouth to the side. "I'm not sure he'll be happy for you to go by yourself. I mean I can try to ask Sergio—"

I raised my hand to stop her. I knew that was bothering her, and I was not here to cause her any undue stress.

"Don't worry. I'll ask him. It's just a quick trip. I'll ask him to take me."

She breathed out with relief, and I felt bad for making her worry even a little.

I rolled my eyes. "He is always teasing me; I want to punch him in the nuts."

She laughed. "Dom has this effect on all of us. He only teases people he likes though. See it as a rite of passage."

"Umph!" I shouldn't care, and yet why did my heart have to leap in my chest at the thought of Dom liking me?

"It will pass. Just don't show him it's annoying. The more he knows it is annoying, the more he will do it."

"Like a boy in sixth grade."

Cassie nodded. "Pretty much."

I sighed, standing up from my spot on her bed. "I'll go find him now, and when we come back, I'll help you pack for the trip, okay?"

"Sure. Can you send Jude in, please, if you see him? I think we need to spend some quality time together."

"Sure thing. Also, what type of sweets would you like?"

"Anything… Wait, no, just some sour Jelly Belly jelly beans and some Skittles… Oh, and some Twizzlers."

"Got it. I'll see you later."

I went downstairs to Jude's room, expecting to find him engrossed in one of his novels, but his door was open and I could hear his voice as well as the deeper, more masculine voice that I knew in a heartbeat was Dom's.

I peeked in discreetly to find Jude standing in front of his mirror in a gray suit, with Dom standing right behind him,

"What do you need then?"

"I'm trying to do my tie, but I can't. Cassie never taught me." He looked up, meeting Dom's eyes in the mirror.

Dom rested his hands on his tapered hips and nodded. "And you want me to teach you?"

Jude nodded.

Dom grinned, and it was as cocky as it could be, once again making my heart leap into my chest. When exactly did I revert back to my teenage self?

"You were right to call me, li'l man. Luca thinks he's good at that, but he is not me. I'll teach you to do the best knots. What do you need that for? D'you have a hot date or something?"

I smiled at that. Dom was so good with Jude.

Jude shook his head, brushing his hand against the blue silk of his tie. "No, the babies will be here soon, and as their uncle I want to make a good first impression on them."

"Hence the suit?"

"Yes."

Dom nodded and knelt down. "Makes sense. Let me show you," he offered, undoing his own black tie.

I had not noticed before how formally he was dressed; he probably had a meeting of some sort.

My heart melted as I kept looking at them and at the patience with which Dom was explaining and showing Jude how to do his tie.

I knew I was way past the point of simply peeking, and I crossed the line of spying like a creep a few minutes ago, but I couldn't help it, seeing that big serious-looking man on his knees explaining to a pretty unique boy how to do his tie... and taking everything just as seriously as Jude was obviously taking it... Lord, it was a surprise that my ovaries had not yet exploded.

"Mobster Lady?"

I jerked back and met Dom's dark gaze in the mirror. "What?"

"He asked you what you wanted?" Jude piped up, his tie now done even if a little crooked.

How long had I zoned out?

"Your sister would like to see you."

"Oh!" He turned around briskly. "I'll change quickly first. I want to keep the suit a surprise."

I nodded and couldn't help but smile as I watched him skip into his bathroom.

I turned to Dom who was refastening his tie. "He's such an amazing little boy."

He nodded. "The best there is."

I could see how much he loved Jude, and that was another sign he was a good man, Mafia or not.

"Did you need anything else? Some snitch you want me to help put in a ditch?"

I rolled my eyes. "When are you going to leave me alone with that?" I asked, trying to convey an annoyance I didn't really feel. I was enjoying the banter; it was so much better than the casual cold shoulder he used to give me.

"Not anytime soon. What is it you need though?"

"I need to go to town; could you please give me a ride?"

He waved his hand dismissively. "Give me a list of what you need. I'll get it."

"No, I really need to go."

He sighed as if I was being difficult. "Listen, whatever you need, I can get it, okay? I'm not that—"

"Tampons, I need tampons. My period came early so if you could get the one with applicators that'd be great. Also, don't take the one for light—"

"Okay, let's go." He looked away and I could not be sure, but it seemed like he faintly blushed under his olive skin. "Be by the car in five minutes," he added, already on his way out of the room.

"Yes, that's what I thought," I muttered behind him, and the way he turned around to glare at me clearly showed that he heard me and was not amused, which strangely enough amused me even more.

If you can give it, you can take it.

––––––––

What I had not expected was standing in the feminine products aisle with big scary Dom standing beside me with his arms crossed, looking at the boxes in front of him with a sort of puzzlement.

"You can go, you know?" I gestured toward the end of the aisle. "I'm sure I can find your giant ass in this store once I'm done."

He arched an eyebrow at me. "Giant ass?" He looked behind him. "Are you serious? My ass is basically made of perfect buns of steel, thank you very much! Squatting is a way of life."

I shrugged. It was true though; his ass was lovely, and I couldn't help but wonder if it was just as firm as it looked. Damn it, I was turning into a perv... No, it was my period; it was messing with my hormones and turning me into a horny teenager.

"No, I'm fascinated." He pointed at the pink and purple box right in front of him. "Do you need them to go horseback riding? Or more to do yoga?" he asked, pointing to another box. "Or maybe you need them to be the businesswoman you are to attend business meetings," he asked with laughter, pointing at a blue box with a woman in a pantsuit smiling while pointing at a chart.

I rolled my eyes. He was right; the boxes were absolutely ridiculous... "Marketing made by men, that's what it is." I muttered to him before reaching for a box on the bottom shelf. "I'd rather buy one that allows multitasking. I can do all of the activities and throw snitches in ditches as well."

His eyes lit with humor as his lips tilted up in the corner in a half smile. He was warming up to me and I loved it.

"Good to know." He looked down the aisle. "Do you need anything else while we're here?"

I shook my head. "No, we'll be in New York in just a few days. I'm sure I can get everything I need there." I had to admit I was excited to go; it was a city I'd always dreamed of visiting but never had the chance.

"Um." He rubbed at his neck, avoiding my eyes. He was not doing that often, but I already came to realize he did it when he was about to say something he knew I wouldn't like.

"What?"

"It's just New York; it's where we have our... *offices*, you know."

"Okay?"

"And it's not as safe as Riverside—much bigger, many enemies."

"I see." I tried not to sound or look disappointed. I came here for Cassie after all and to get away from Calgary for a while. I didn't come to be a tourist.

He sighed. "I'll be busy with work because Luca won't have much time and—"

"It's okay. Don't worry about it. I'll just stay in." I shrugged. "I understand, really."

Dom studied me silently, and somehow I got lost in his inquisitive brown eyes as if we were not in the middle of the hygiene aisle of the small local supermarket but under the stars somewhere, just the two of us.

"I'll find a way; I'll take you around town," he said, his voice a little breathless. He seemed rattled enough to let me hope that I had an effect on him too.

"Dom, I—" We were interrupted by my phone ringing. I got it out of my pocket, and everything stopped at the name flashing on my screen. *'Jake,'* a name I thought and hoped I'd never see again.

Ice settled in the pit of my stomach as I kept staring at my screen, too shocked to even reject the call. Did he really think there was a chance of me ever picking up his call? Did he not know I had passed the point of ever caring, of ever forgiving?

I could feel my body ache where my bones had been broken. I slid my tongue out, subconsciously running it over my bottom lip where it had been split.

It could not be true, not now. The phone finally stopped ringing, and the name vanished from my screen, somehow easing the steel vise around my lungs.

"Who's Jake?"

I jerked my head up, having forgotten for a second where I was and who I was with.

Dom was glowering down at the phone I was holding like it had personally offended him. *My worst and most painful mistake.* "No one."

He looked up, his face softening almost immediately. "India..." He sighed wearily.

I shrugged and turned around, breaking eye contact. "We all have a past, don't we? We all have secrets." And Lord knew he probably had a million of those.

"Yes, but the difference is my secret won't hurt you."

I frowned. "I assure you, my secret won't hurt you either. I'll be back. I need some *stuff*," I finished rather lamely. I just needed to be away from him right now; he was messing with my resolve.

"Of course they will. If they hurt you, they hurt me."

I just stopped walking and stared at him. "What?"

"*Us*, they hurt *us*. You're part of the family and we protect our family." He cleared his throat. "Go get what you need. I'll meet you at the register. I realized I need something too," he replied quickly before turning around briskly and disappearing down the other side of the aisle.

What the hell was that? How could he not realize how his words affected me?

He'd just made this declaration and kept on going like nothing happened, like he hadn't just admitted something that changed so many things between us. He just admitted that I mattered.

I shook my head, picked up the few things I needed, and met Dom by the registers.

I almost had to laugh at seeing him standing there in his dark suit, his arms crossed on his chest, and what seemed to be a very constant glower in his eyes.

Maybe it was the male equivalent of the bitch resting face. I needed to look into that.

But despite the air of danger and dominance coming off of him in waves, the few housewives shopping around in the daytime in their classic yoga pants and high ponytails kept throwing him looks full of lust, and that really grated me the wrong way.

What's wrong with you, India McKenna? That man is not yours! You have no right to feel territorial.

"You're done?" he asked when I reached him with my basket full of crap I didn't really need. I just needed a few moments to compose myself both because of my conflicting feelings for him and Jake's call.

I nodded. "I thought you needed something too."

He shook his head. "I changed my mind." He reached for the basket in my hand and just the brush of his warm calloused fingers on my hand made me shiver. "Let me take care of this."

"I'll pay!" I said, reaching in my handbag.

He rested his hand on top of mine, the first real conscious touch between us. I looked up and saw his pupils dilate. Yes, there was no doubt I was affecting him too and he was fighting it probably even harder than I was. Why?

"I pay, don't start," he commanded, tightening his hold on the basket handle.

"Okay." Did my voice sound as breathless as I heard? Lord, kill me now.

I let him take the basket and take care of every-thing. I waited by the door, looking at the candy store across the road as I thought of all the reasons why having an infatuation for Dom the Mafia guy was a very bad idea.

One, he clearly had issues and I was not talking about a small sports bag. No, he was clearly carrying a set of ten giant suitcases. Two, well... *Mafia*. That in itself should have me running in the opposite direc-tion. Three, I ran from Calgary for a reason, and it was not to fall in the arms of a damaged, dangerous man, and four—and I could not stress this one enough—I was convinced that this man, if I let myself go, would break me beyond repair.

"I never thought the candy store was so fascinating."

I startled back to reality to find Dom standing beside me, a brown bag in his arms.

"Cassie asked me to get her a few things. I was thinking about what to get."

"Of course she did." He rolled his eyes before turning around and walking slowly toward the exit. "I swear I don't know how that woman can stay so small with all the sugar she is ingesting. Don't over-think it; just buy anything with sugar. That's what I do."

"Oh, you got another love note," I joked as we reached his car and I noticed the piece of white paper stuck to his wiper.

Dom looked around, his jaws tight, his eyes like hawks trying to zoom in on their prey. "Yes, crazy soccer moms can be clingy..." He trailed off absent-mindedly, still scanning the almost empty street.

I wanted to diffuse the atmosphere; I wanted the carefree Dom again. "That's the problem when you give a good dick."

His dark eyebrows shot up in surprise. I enjoyed that, taking him by surprise. I was not what he expected and somehow it pushed me to be myself more and more around him.

He recovered his cocky facade quite fast and let out a derisive snort. "Please, I don't give good dick. I give *amazing* dick!"

Don't say it, don't say it, don't— "I'm a scientist, Dom. I believe what can be proven—maybe we should experiment." *I'd said it.* At least I could take comfort in the fact that my tone still sounded amused. This could very much be put on the count of banter. But I knew the ugly truth, deep down. If that man was to enter my room in the middle of the night, I would not send him away.

He threw me a look that seemed to be part longing, part sadness, not really something I expected after basically throwing myself at him.

"Why don't you go to the store and pick stuff for Cassie. I'll put the bag in the car and meet you there."

"Okay." I took a couple of steps off the sidewalk before turning toward him. "You're okay, right?"

"Of course I am. Why wouldn't I be?" He smiled, but even if I barely knew him, I knew it was fake. "I just need to make sure I blame the new sugar delivery on you so Luca won't kill me like he threatened to do."

I nodded and turned around. He was hiding something; of course he was. He was hiding many things, in fact, but somehow this one bothered me because even if I didn't admit it to myself, I didn't like to see him preoccupied. I could not ask Cassie about it; she was already worrying much more than she should.

As for Luca, what could I even ask? It could bring

nothing up, and then Dom would be upset with me for looking into him.

I sighed, walking into the colorful store, the smell of sugar hitting my nostrils and somehow making me feel a little better.

I looked out the window to see Dom close the trunk of his car and go to the front, ripping the note from under his wiper and reading it before tightening it in his fist and putting it in his pants pocket.

I'll discover your secret, Dom, I vowed as he crossed the street to come meet me. *And maybe then I'll tell you mine.*

DOM

"Did you want to see me?" I asked, entering Luca's office.

He nodded, leaning back on his chair, a glass of scotch in his hand. It was funny how eighteen months could make a difference. I knew that this was Luca's first drink of the day, his way to unwind for a while from the pressure of his capo role and the risky pregnancy of the love of his life. Before I would have wondered how far he had been down the bottle because the further he was, the meaner he got.

He gestured me toward the seat across from him.

"Don't think I don't know what you're doing."

I froze. I was doing a lot, and some of it I knew he

would not approve. Especially the notes I've been receiving. I wanted to tell him; I should have told him. The note at the airport was one thing. It could even be a fluke or just someone trying to stir shit, but here it was home, our safe haven, and the note was much more specific, much more real. '*Innocence thief*', but he was so worried about everything, how could I add to his worry? It would make me a bad friend and a bad consigliere.

I would tell him, I tried to convince myself. Once the babies were here, I'd tell him.

"What are you talking about?"

"Everything you're doing for me; you're taking on much more than you should have."

I relaxed in my seat. "I'm your consigliere, Luca. This is what I'm here for."

He gave me a small smile. "No, not that much. Matteo told me you're going to work with him in New York, and I know how you feel about him."

Weirdly enough, the more time I spent with Genovese, the less I disliked him. He was still a crazy psycho—nothing would change that—but somehow it was not such a hardship anymore. "To be fair, it's not that bad. I'm even planning a girls' night. I'll braid his hair; he'll paint my nails."

Luca chuckled. "Is everything okay, Dom, really?"

I sighed, looking away for a second. Luca was not an idiot. If he asked that now, it was because he knew the truth, or at least part of it. He was attuned to me.

"I'm not certain," I admitted. "Matteo is hell-bent on burning the world to the ground to find the rat, and I agree we need to find him." Even more now than before, I thought as the nameless notes came to the front of my mind. "But he is getting deeper into the Russian and Albanian world, not a scene we're familiar with."

Luca nodded, tracing the scar on his cheek idly. "Normally I would agree; these are troubled waters at best, but this is Matteo we're talking about. He's as smart as he is cunning and probably more vicious and dangerous than any of them."

"He is something."

"He'll keep you safe."

"I don't need him to keep me safe."

"I know you don't, but Matteo can and will go to some length that both of us would hardly consider... having a conscience and all."

"Do you ever feel bad for the woman he'll have to marry?"

Matteo Genovese was Mafia royalty. Well, he was our king here in the US, as high as you could be. If the rules of having an heir were strongly suggested to us here, it had to be mandatory for him.

"Daily... Talking about women, I couldn't help but notice that things are getting better between you and India."

God, for a capo, Luca was sometimes as subtle as an elephant in a China shop.

"She's living here, and she is okay." I shrugged. "I'm making do of the situation."

"She's lovely. I like her."

I was not entirely sure where he was going with it. A little pinch of pain squeezed my heart at the possible meaning of his words. Was he trying to tell me he was protecting her from me? Like I would even dare soil this good woman with what I was.

"Don't worry, Luca. I don't intend to get closer to her."

"I'm not—" He groaned with a frustrated huff. "That is not at all where I was going with this. Dom, there's—"

"Did you send her to speak with Jude?" I interrupted, so done with where the conversation was going. "I saw them in the greenhouse before."

Luca shrugged. "Based on Google, she's quite amazing at her job. He's saying he is happy, but I just want to make sure, you know? The life he has now is so different from what he's used to. I love the kid."

I nodded. His worry was resonating with me. The kid really made his place in our hearts. "What's not to love? The kid is amazing just like Cassie." I stood up and helped myself to a drink. "How did people like them have kids like that is beyond me." I took a sip of the drink, walking to the window and looking at the garden full of flowers—something Cassie created, bringing both literal and metaphoric light into our lives.

"These people are serial killers, sociopaths." He met my eyes. "You're not your parents, Dom."

I shrugged. "Some are more than others."

"You are *not* your father."

"Not completely," I agree but some of his evilness, his viciousness ran through my veins.

"Not at all," Luca insisted.

I sighed. "Do they know about their parents?" Luca promised them safety if they agreed to sign their parental rights away, allowing him to adopt Jude, but the more he realized the extent of their neglect, the less he could keep his word, and they had finally been taken out a couple of months back.

"Cassie does. I'm not hiding anything from my wife—ever."

I turned toward him, leaning my shoulder against the wall. "How did she take it?"

"She felt guilty to have caused a black mark on my soul." He barked a small humorless laugh. "I don't think she realizes how many marks are already there —One more means nothing at all."

"What about the kid, does he know?"

Luca shook his head. "No, Cassie and I thought it was better to keep that for us. They don't deserve him even sparing one more thought to them."

I took a slow sip of my drink. "I think you did well to have India talk to him; she is kind and perceptive. If anyone can read him, it's her."

Luca pressed his forefinger against his lips as the corner lifted a little.

"What?" I asked subconsciously. It was really not a subject worth laughing about.

"You know, it's okay to like her."

"I don't like her," I barked. *Fuck!* I replied too fast, too vehemently. I felt like I was back in school again.

Luca's smile grew a little. Yeah, he didn't miss that.

"Oh we're doing the all 'in denial' thing? Okay."

I rolled my eyes. "What are we? Back in high school?"

"You tell me. I've already told my prom queen I loved her, and I've put my babies in her." He gestured toward me. "You're the one acting all brooding and mysterious. 'I like you but stay away from me' type of weird vampire dude."

"Vampire dude?" I ask, narrowing my eyes in suspicion. "Lord, don't tell me you watched *Twilight* again."

Luca slumped back on his seat. "It's Cassie. I swear her pregnancy is getting her all weird. That was what we did last night in bed."

"I see…" I couldn't help the mischievous smile appearing on my face. Poking fun at Luca was much safer territory than the beautiful psychologist that was forcing her way into my head. "How exciting is married life! Watching movies about brooding

108

vampires and teenage werewolves... Let me guess, you ate popcorn too?"

Luca snorted. "That's preposterous! We did no such thing!"

"Cereal?"

"Lucky Charms."

We burst into laughter. I loved these moments of carefree friendship we had despite their rarity. There were moments I never thought I'd ever get back when Luca sank into depression after his mother and sister's deaths, but he was back now, and once again that was thanks to Cassie, who saved him and in the same line, me, in more ways than she'd ever know.

"Thank you. I needed that." He relaxed in his seat, and I realized how tense he had been before our little banter.

I take a sip of my drink, studying my friend, and I notice more and more the little details that show the extent of his weariness. His dark circles, visible despite the darker hue of his olive skin, the taut skin around his eyes and mouth...

"You know everything is fine, right?"

He nodded but remained silent.

"Listen, Cassie is followed by the most prestigious OB-GYN on the East Coast and the issue of the rat I'm dealing with."

"That's the thing though, isn't it?" he said so quietly I was not sure it was for me.

I frowned, walking closer to him. "What is?"

"You shouldn't have to be the one dealing with all that. It is my responsibility. My kingdom."

I let out a humorless little laugh. "Uneasy is the head that wears a crown."

"Quoting Henry IV?" He pursed his lips in an impressed pout. "Nice."

"That's all on the kid." I waved my hand dismissively. "The thing is, Luca Henry IV was a narcissistic ass. You need to share that weight with me, like you shared mine for so many years."

Luca had been the one who took me in after my father was killed; he had been the one keeping the secret of all the atrocities I'd done and witnessed. He did all of this at only fourteen years old. He'd fought the council, his father... anyone, like a wolf protecting his pack, and it had all been for me.

How could he ever think that any sacrifice or task would ever be too much? He deserved this and so much more. I owed him everything.

"You were never a weight for me, Domenico."

"Same here."

He sighed, running his hands on his face wearily. "Yes, I know. You're a protector like I am."

"Of my family? Yes. The rest"—I shrugged—"can get lost."

"And does this family include India?"

"Who's Jake?" I asked, purposely dodging the question, but the temptation was much too great.

"What do you mean?"

110

"She's been getting calls... She rejects them but she's different after that—more distant, worried."

"And it rubs you the wrong way? To have her distancing herself?"

He was still fishing for information; I could totally imagine him and Cassie talking behind our backs like two old *nonnas* in church.

"It's more a concern of any potential threat, really. She seems nervous and dodges questions... That's a red flag, and as you said before, I'm the protector of my family."

He twisted his mouth to the side; it was not really the answer he hoped for.

"I'm not sure who Jake is, but I think he may have a part to play in India coming here," he admitted. "I know my wife by heart and she's a protector. It's not like Cassie to involve someone in our lives. By allowing India to come into our circle, she was always risking her discovering the truth and therefore being a target in some way. I just don't think she did it without some serious forethought."

I nodded, trying to rein in my urge to kill this man, whoever he was, for hurting what was mine.

Yours? Fuck, are you crazy?! That woman will never be yours.

Truth was India managed to wake my body in ways that softness never did before. My cock hardened to her softness. It almost felt like I was not broken, like I could be saved, and this was the worst.

She was waking up a part of me that I thought only responded to pain and fear... and that both intrigued and terrified me. Part of me wanted to hope that maybe if I tried with her, things could be different, but it was too dangerous to hope—it cost too much.

"Cassie won't tell me much either," Luca continued, somehow clueless of my internal turmoil, something that I was grateful for.

"Your wife is the most faithful, trustworthy woman I've ever met. It's not a pick and choose quality that you know. If we love her being like that with us, we can't blame her for being like that with everyone else."

Luca rolled his eyes. "It's infuriating when it's not to my advantage."

I let out a low chuckle. "I bet it is."

He leaned back on his seat and crossed his arms on his chest. "I know my time will be otherwise occupied when we're in the city, but I'd like for you to run down your program for me. I know what Matteo said, but you're my consigliere. There's no one in our circle I trust more than you."

This meant so much more to me than he could ever imagine. Luca's trust had been what kept me going for so long, what kept the blackness in me at bay.

I told him about the places Matteo wanted me to go and the two meetings I was supposed to attend, but I did something that showed me that India meant much more to me than I even expected. I didn't tell him about my plan to show her the city.

I was not ready to share this because I didn't even know what it meant for me or for her.

But for now I just need to find out who was the rat and forget the beautiful doctor occupying my mind.

8

DOM

"How are you?" I asked Jude as he tapped his foot rhythmically against the ugly lime-green linoleum in the hospital waiting room.

He stopped tapping his foot. "It bothers you? Cassie says some people get annoyed by it but..." He shrugged his frail shoulder. "I do that. I don't know why."

I slid to the chair closer to his and rested my hand on his shoulder. I looked down at my hand, how massive it looked on his small frame. This boy needed to be protected at all costs.

"It doesn't bother me; you can tap away. I just want to make sure you're okay."

"Yes, I think so," he replied with a certain uncertainty, his eyes still locked on the ugly floor.

Not really the answer I was going for but that would have to do. I was not good at pushing him; I was more the kind to let him know I was here and open to chat whenever he felt like he wanted to.

I started to tap my own foot, a welcome distraction. "We can even do a concerto if you want."

Jude gave me a little side smile and it made me feel better. I helped him, this sweet little innocent boy. I couldn't be as bad, as rotten as that if I managed that.

"Any space for a third one?"

My heart shamefully skipped a beat at the mere sound of her voice. I looked up, hoping my face looked emotionless despite the turmoil she caused in me.

She smiled at me when I met her eyes and the vise on my lungs started to squeeze. This woman was a witch.

Jude looked down at her feet, twisting his mouth to the side, seriously considering her question.

I did my best not to pull the boy into a hug. His way of taking everything so literal made him so endearing.

"You're wearing flat ballet pumps; I'm not sure it will work."

She nodded. "You're right." Her tone mirrored his seriousness. She jerked the carton drink tray under his nose. "What about if I bribe you with a hot chocolate?"

Jude keyed up, "Sure," He took the drink she handed him. "But I'd say yes anyway, you know."

She chuckled. "I do." She handed me a small cup. "Double shot macchiato, one sugar."

I couldn't hide my surprise when I took the cup from her.

"What?" she asked, taking the seat beside me.

"No, nothing. It's just—" I shook my head before taking a sip of the coffee goodness. I was praying it would do miracles on my sleep-deprived brain.

Today was Cassie's planned C-section. I'd barely slept all night, first, because I was worried for her, and second, because I was cooped up in Luca's condo with India only a door away without any supervision and that had been harder than I anticipated.

"I'm just interested. I remember things you say." She shrugged. "No big deal."

"Yeah," I replied, looking down at my cup lid, but she was wrong. It *was* a big deal. Except for Luca and Cassie, she was the first person to show me genuine interest without having any ulterior motive. She didn't need my power, my skills, my money, or my dick...

I threw her a side-glance as she looked away thoughtfully, running her long, slender forefinger around the rim of her cup.

Maybe she did want my dick. Part of me hoped

she did, that she was as aware of me as I was of her and that she, too, touched herself with me in mind.

"No?"

I refocused on her, slightly startled. I had not heard a word she'd said.

I cocked my head to the side, shrugging a little. "I see your point." That was a catch-all answer I'd used so many times before.

She cocked one of her perfectly shaped eyebrows. "You see my point?" she asked, a smile tugging at the corner of her plump berry-colored lips. Would they be as soft and tasty as they looked? I could almost feel her bottom lip between my lips as I nibbled it gently.

I swallowed as my dick twitched at the mere thought. It was so not the place or the time, but it was also so unexpected. My body only responded to force, pain, submission... How could the thought of her lips, doing something as chaste as kissing me, set ablaze my body in such a way?

"You didn't hear a word I said, did you?" she chastised, but the laughter in her voice softened the blow.

I gave her a sheepish smile and was about to answer, to give her some harmless flirting banter when we were interrupted by a guest I never expected in the maternity ward waiting room of this private women's health hospital.

"Genovese?" I sat straighter, suddenly alerted by his presence in the room with India and Jude. I didn't like her being close to him at all. "What do you need?"

He gave us his cocky smile, the one he wanted to be jovial, even a little flirty, but it didn't reach his eyes. I guess it was hard to fake when you were dead inside.

"Rude, Domenico," he said with a small shake of his head. "You could at least introduce me to your lovely company." He smiled even brighter and bowed a little at the waist. "I'm Matteo Genovese, nice to meet you."

India was like frozen beside me. She didn't look enticed like most women were when they looked at him. No, she was wary. She was smart.

"I'm India, Cassie's cousin."

"Indeed, you are." He turned toward Jude. *"Come stai Giuda? Come ti stai divertendo in collegio?"*

Jude studied Matteo silently like he always did, as if he could recognize something in him. Was it Matteo's sociopathy that was calling to Jude's Asperger's?

Finally, Jude gave him a little nod. *"Sto bene. La scuola è un po 'troppo facile per me. Ma almeno ho gli scacchi."*

Matteo laughed and nodded, visibly impressed.

I was impressed too. Jude was not born into our world, and yet his Italian was almost perfect. It was also strange how he could talk so freely about school and chess with the boss of the bosses, and what was even stranger was that Matteo liked the kid.

"Was there anything you needed?" I asked him, trying to redirect his attention to me. I really didn't like him near anyone I cared about.

"Just wanted to see how things were going. You know, the babies and all. It will be good to have a Montanari heir for the famiglia."

He glanced at India's face, who didn't look surprised, and a glint lit his cold blue eyes. He now knew that she knew. Calculating bastard.

"Makes sense." No, it didn't. "I'll text you if you want; you don't have to wait here."

His nostrils flared as his jaw muscle budged. He did not like my answer.

"*È successo qualcosa. Dobbiamo andare. Adesso,*" he ordered in Italian, his voice much colder now; he was letting go of pretenses.

India frowned, looking at him. She didn't have to understand Italian to know what he said wasn't pleasant.

What could be so important for him to need me to follow him now?

I turned to India, really conflicted. I wanted to be there with them. I wanted to share that moment with my family, but I also knew that saying no to Matteo Genovese would have consequences not only on me but on Luca as well.

India smiled sweetly at me and rested her hand on

my thigh. "You do what you need to," she said softly, patting my thigh. "I'll explain you had to go. They'll understand."

Was it possible to fall in love at once? Because right now as I felt her warm hand on my leg and looked in her mesmerizing green eyes, I felt like I was falling from a cliff.

"Okay, now, let's go."

I blinked, somehow brought back to the now by Matteo's unwelcome voice.

I shot up from my chair, still a little startled by the wave of feelings that had engulfed me all at once.

"Just—" I started and stopped, looking at the stunning woman in front of me like a loon.

She smiled. "I'll text you as soon as I have news."

I gave her a sharp nod before following Matteo down the corridor.

"I truly hope it's important," I muttered as the elevator closed on us.

He threw me a sideways look. "Do you really think I would have pulled you away for something that would not be crucial?"

Of course I did! Matteo never cared about anything other than what was in his own interest. "Like you care."

He shrugged. "I really don't, but you do."

That startled me and I almost missed a step as we exited the elevator. There was no way Matteo Genovese cared about what I thought or wanted. He was much too selfish and frankly messed up for that. He was playing with my mind; there was no other way.

I snorted. "Oh yeah, because what I think or feel matters now?"

He sighed with exasperation. "No, not really but I need you right now, and I need you receptive and on my side, and the best way to do this is to show you a modicum of consideration—or so I have been told."

I couldn't help but let out a little chuckle. That made so much more sense.

"So, the girl..." He trailed off as we sat in his car.

I didn't even realize I let out a growl until he threw me a surprised look before starting the engine.

"Down, boy. No need to growl at me. The girl's not my type. She's all yours."

It was my turn to throw him an incredulous look. "Yes, sure, model-like stunning isn't your type." I shook my head.

"Actually, it isn't. I like them much shorter and much curvier."

I was surprised, not because of his statement per se. Tastes came in all shapes and forms, but somehow I didn't expect him to have a type. I saw him as the kind of man who just needed a woman to relieve his bodily needs on a purely physiological level.

A bit like me... Well, no, I had a type; the woman in the hospital was my type, but for my twisted desires? Anyone who would take what I give them, not as a trauma, was good enough for me .

I took a deep breath, shaking off any reminder of my conflicting feelings for India. Now was not the time. I was with Genovese; I had to keep my head in the game.

"Where are we going?"

"Baker's Place."

I grimaced. That had to be important. There were the bad areas in town. There were the terrible parts of town, and then there was Baker's Place... It was the dumpiest dump in dumpsville. Even rats were scared to catch rabies there.

"Did you get all your vaccines? Your tetanus shot?" I asked, not even sure I was joking.

He cracked his neck to the side, visibly irritated. I was not sure if it was me or the situation that was getting on his nerves, probably a mix of both.

"The Living Ghost is there."

I turned sharply on my seat to look at him. "What?" He'd been hunting the man for weeks, almost to the point of obsession, and he just let that out so casually. "How?"

"Volkov," he simply said as if this word alone explained everything, but it really didn't.

This name actually caused more questions. Russians and Italians had never been close, never been allies. We sometimes helped each other when newcomers were trying to steal what we took years to acquire but it never went further. We'd never turn our back to a Russian and yet our king was colluding with one of their most volatile princes.

"What do you have on him?"

"I told you, the girl."

I threw him a doubtful look.

He sighed. "I found her and brought her back to him, unharmed."

"You found her? Was she taken?" I sometimes forgot that there was another reason for me not getting involved with India. If I did, I would not be the only threat in her life.

"Not exactly. She was confused, so I brought her back to her rightful place."

I raised my eyebrows. "Genovese... Did you kidnap a poor girl for a Russian mobster?"

He waved a hand dismissively, "Kidnap is a big word. It's all a matter of perception."

"It's so fucking not."

He threw me a sideways look. "She should have known better than being involved with him. He assured me he would not hurt her before I handed her to him though. I'm not a complete monster."

Aren't you?

"They seemed okay the last time I saw him; he probably dicked her into submission."

I winced but didn't have time to add anything as Matteo parked in front of a decrepit building that looked like a pit stop for crack addicts. It was absolutely charming if you wished to catch a deathly disease just by breathing.

"He's living there?"

I turned to Matteo who was looking at the building with a disgusted pout which I was sure matched my own.

"I guess it's fitting for a ghost," I added, trying to lighten the atmosphere.

Matteo turned to me, his blue eyes shining with his murderous rage. "Let's finish this."

I followed him into the building and the piss smell almost made me gag. I looked at the overused, holey floorboard, the flaking walls, the exposed electrical wires.

"Charming... I can almost smell the asbestos," I whispered as Matteo walked down the narrow corridor. I was grateful we didn't have to take the stairs as, based on how they looked, there was no way they could support men of our height and weight.

Matteo stopped in front of the door of what used to be apartment two if I believed the discoloration on the door.

Matteo retrieved his gun from his holster and cocked it before jerking his head toward the door, his silent command for me to take it down; I was the muscles after all.

I rolled my eyes and gestured him to move out of the way. Matteo was not a small man; he could have easily done it himself, but I was sure he didn't want to wrinkle his designer suit.

I took a step back and kicked the door open in just one half-assed try.

As soon as the door hit the floor, Matteo walked in, his gun up. That was reckless of him to walk in first but he was on a warpath.

I followed close behind him and what I saw I didn't expect.

A man, who I suspected was the 'living ghost' was dead—very, very dead. He was sitting, or rather slouching, on a chair, a clean shot in the middle of his forehead, the dark drying blood cacking his blond hair.

I let my eyes trail down his arm and his hand, still holding his fully burned cigarette which left burns on his fingers.

My eyes went back up to the note taped to his chest on his white wifebeater.

'Too late.'

"*Figlio di puttana!*" Matteo roared in furor, reaching for the camping table the man was sitting at, throwing it at the other side of the room where it fell, legs up.

He turned to me, his face, usually so stoic, was beet red, the veins on his neck bulging to a point it looked like they were about to burst.

"How?" he shouted at me. "*Fanculo!* I found out

two hours ago!" He turned around and kicked the chair, making the body fall to the floor.

I was speechless, watching him pace the length of the room, rambling in Italian.

I'd never seen Matteo lose his cool like that. He had never slipped. I had seen glimpses of the man behind the cool, collected veneer but never anything close to this.

"This is impossible!" he shouted again, running his hand in his hair, messing up his usually perfect style.

"Maybe we should ask for help."

He turned around briskly. "*Sei pazzo?*"

"No, I'm not crazy. The rat is clearly much better than we thought." I pointed at the body lying on the floor. "That guy made money being a ghost his whole life, and yet he didn't even get to fight; he trusted his attacker. The traitor is good. We might need to ask for help fr—"

Matteo shook his head. "No!"

I frowned. "Matteo, listen."

"I said no, Domenico." His cold voice lashed like a whip. "How do you think it will look to have a rat in our ranks?" He shook his head again, his dark hair falling on his forehead. "I'm the youngest capo dei capi; you're one of the first made men to become consigliere, and Gianluca is probably the most progressive capo there is. How do you think it will reflect on you? On me?"

I pursed my lips. Fuck, I hated to admit he was right. Some more traditional members had not welcomed Matteo's arrival, and it was also true that some of Luca's decisions were received with high skepticism.

I sighed. "So what do we do?"

Matteo went eerily still, looking down at the body on the floor. He put his gun back in his holster and rearranged his hair, his face back to the stoic placid facade I'd always known.

It had been unsettling to see him flip the switch from placid sociopath to angry psycho and back to placid sociopath in less than ten minutes.

"We search this motherfucking dump for any clue whatsoever, then we bleach our fucking hands so as not to catch whatever hell this place may carry and we go on our merry way."

I raised an eyebrow suspiciously. "And that's it?"

He laughed. "No, of course not, then we raise havoc to snuffle that rat out, and once we do..." He turned to me and grinned. "It'll be my time to shine."

His grin caused chills down my back; it was sadistic—a twisted grin promising all kinds of pain.

I looked at the table and frowned before crouching and retrieving the white envelope stuck at the bottom.

"Like this maybe..." I ripped the envelope from under the table and reached for what was in it. "A key," I said, grabbing it between my thumb and forefinger, showing it to Matteo.

It was just a generic silver deposit box key with no real distinctive signs except for a number on one side that said 6734.

"A deposit box key," Matteo commented, mirroring my own assessment.

I nodded, putting it in my pocket.

"Let's keep on going," Matteo ordered, already walking into the next room.

I highly doubted there would be more to find in that dump. To be fair the key itself seemed like a miracle, even if truth be told there were deposit boxes all over the city and it could even be from another state... It was a long shot but it was all we had.

I was going through his kitchen cabinets, which were low on food but overwhelmingly high in cockroaches.

"Fucking vermin," I spat in disgust as one crawled on my hand.

I shook it off as my phone vibrated in my pocket.

I retrieved it and smiled, my sour mood vanishing at India's name flashing on my screen.

It was just a simple text and a photo.

'Babies and mom are doing great. Dad is frazzled but still standing.' I chuckled and opened the photo of the two infants, wrapped like burritos and sleeping in clear plastic beds.

"What are you laughing at?"

I turned toward Matteo who was standing beside the body like nothing was there.

I flipped my phone and showed him the photo. "The babies are here; everybody is doing well."

He nodded. "Bene, one last thing to worry about; the Montanari line will keep on going."

I rolled my eyes. Leave it to Matteo to be pragmatic even at this moment.

I shot her a quick thank-you text before concentrating on Matteo again.

"*Andiamo.*" He jerked his head toward the exit. "We won't find anything more and I don't want to stand here when they find him... or when the rats will come to feed."

Bile rose in my throat at the thought and at the memory. I'd seen that before and it was even grosser than anyone could imagine.

"*Si.*" I was just eager to leave this pest-infested building.

Once we sat in the car, Matteo relaxed a little and leaned back against his seat.

"Let's forget about before; it's not in my habits to let people see that..."

"You're human?" I offered.

He threw me a glare. "Those things have the ability to get to me."

"I get it. It would affect the most patient man.

We've been working on that for months and we don't have anything."

"I wouldn't say that. Actually, we have a lot more than you might think."

"The key to a safety deposit box?" I took the key out of my pocket and held it in my palm. "There's no distinctive sign about this key—only a number."

"True, but we'll find it and that man was not an idiot. He lived hidden too well, for far too long. You noticed it, didn't you?"

He was testing me; everything was a test with Matteo.

"He didn't fight."

His eyes lit up and there was approval there. Why would he even care about what I noticed or not. It was not like I was his consigliere... Matteo didn't even have one; he was above it.

"Exactly, meaning that he didn't see the person, the *Mano Vendicativa*," he spat with disgust, "as an actually threat."

"Okay, so you think..." I trailed off.

"I think it might be a woman."

That made me jerk back in surprise. "A woman?"

"Why not? Women can be just as smart as men and certainly way more vindictive."

That statement right there was so progressist that it would make the families frown. Women were not supposed to be as smart as men. For the old-school

Cosa Nostra, a woman could not outsmart a man…
What a bunch of fools.

"The guy you tortured said the voice sounded male."

Matteo shrugged. "It's easy to find a way to change your voice."

"That's true. I've got an app I use when I get bored, and I prank call men from the famiglia."

Matteo looked at me speechlessly, his mouth slightly ajar, his eyebrows raised in surprise. "You're… prank calling people? You're thirty-five, Domenico."

I shrugged. "Thirty-four, and I'm not doing it that much anymore, but when I'm bored? *Perchè no?*"

Matteo burst into laughter, and I couldn't remember the last time I saw him laugh like that. Honestly I didn't think he ever did.

"That's the best thing I've heard all year!" He wiped under his eyes. "Wait a minute." He turned toward me, his eyes narrowed in suspicion. "Are you the one who kept calling my cell for Sex-express?"

"Get a mind-blowing blow job in less than thirty minutes?" I grinned. "I was quite proud of that one."

Matteo growled, pinching the bridge of his nose. "I should shoot you in the kneecaps for that."

"You should… but you won't. You still need me."

He sighed. "It's annoyingly accurate."

He grabbed the key from my hand. "We'll find out what it opens; I can assure you of that." He took a deep breath, leaning his head against his headrest. "Let's go to The Rectory. I need a drink."

I looked at my watch. Visiting hours at the hospital were over, so I couldn't go see Cassie and the babies before tomorrow anyway.

"Is The Rectory really the best for a drink? It's not their main purpose."

Matteo threw me a side-look before starting the car. "I was not thinking about that type of drink, Domenico, but more fucking our day's frustration away. You can have the lovely Elodie for the night; I know how fond you are of her."

I nodded silently as we exited Baker's Place. Maybe going to The Rectory and having Elodie would help me think straighter. Maybe it would reduce my obsession with India and I could rationalize again and stop myself from doing anything stupid like sucking her up into my messed-up life.

I should have known better...

INDIA

I looked dreamily at all the tubs of ice cream in the freezer, thanking whichever god for Luca's house-keeper skills.

I had the condo all to myself tonight. Jude was out with Luca's cousin, Enzo. Luca decided to spend the night at the hospital, unable to leave his family's side, and Dom texted me an hour ago saying he had plans for the evening and not to wait for him.

I grabbed the sharing tub of ice cream... 'Sharing.' What a joke! I never shared ice cream.

I removed the cover, grabbed a big spoon, and stabbed it in the choco-mint goodness.

I needed to indulge tonight for so many reasons.

One because seeing Luca holding his children with such care, looking at Cassie with so much love and adoration made my ovaries scream with envy. It was strange that a big, scary man like Luca turned out to be Prince Charming disguised as a beast and not the other way around, which was unfortunately more common. Cassie had no chance resisting it.

Would Dom be like that too? I shook my head. I needed to stop focusing on Dom and my attraction to him, but I knew he was a good man, no matter what his job was. Mafia didn't mean monster.

A shiver ran down my spine at the thought of the man I met in the waiting room... Maybe he was one. His coldness, his lack of emotion hidden under his perfect beautiful veneer had given me chills. He reminded me of my case study on serial killers.

I growled. *Sure, be an idiot, India, thinking about serial killers when you're alone in one of the biggest cities in the world...*

I put a spoonful of ice cream in my mouth just as my phone started to vibrate to an unknown number. I just stared at it until it stopped ringing. I knew who it was... Jake. I finally decided to block his number. I was tired of it all, but he now called me with a lot of different numbers. The next step was to change my number, but it was such a hassle to do from the US. I had been so clear though, after what he did to me, after the police got involved. How could he ever think I would speak to him again? I touched my eye socket and winced at the phantom pain. No, never again.

Three years we'd been together, two of them were mostly in pain and abuse, both physically and mentally. I was ashamed sometimes, ashamed to have fallen for all his tricks, his beautiful words. I was supposed to be smarter than that; I was a psychologist! I'd seen this situation through my patients' eyes so many times before. I knew the signs. I'd seen the red flags—his desire to control me, his constant putting me down—but my need to be loved had been so strong. I put all that aside thinking it was just a different kind of love. But it wasn't. It had been a narcissistic, egotistical evil man wanting to own me. I was lucky I realized it just in time. So many other poor women didn't.

I exited the kitchen with my gigantic tub of ice cream and froze when the door of the condo opened to reveal Dom.

"I thought you were coming back late," I accused him, mortified at him seeing me in this state.

He raised his eyebrows in surprise.

I wriggled my feet, looking down at my over-sized gray sweatpants and ugly, well-worn orange 'University of Calgary' t-shirt. If I'd known there was a chance he could be back before I went to bed…

I reached up and touched the bird's nest-looking bun on top of my head. *Lord help me.*

"Sorry?" He looked me up and down, from my bare feet to the hideous hairdo.

God, did I remove the spot patch I'd put on my chin earlier?

"No, it's just—you caught me off guard. You said you would be home really late." I brought my hand up to my chin as discreetly as possible and felt the piece of plastic on it. I wished for the floor to just swallow me whole.

He buried his hands in his pants pockets, still studying me with a half smile, obviously enjoying both my discomfort and disheveled state. *Asshole.*

He nodded. "I did say that, but it turned out I was not interested in the evening plans anymore."

"I see. So you'd rather spend your evening with this mess." I pointed at myself.

His grin widened. "Hot mess."

I rolled my eyes but I couldn't help the wave of pleasure at his words even if I knew he was joking. No one could find me attractive like this.

"Was I interrupting a hot date or something?" he asked, walking into the room, removing his jacket, and putting it on the back of a dining table chair.

"Yep, I was about to spend my evening with Chris Hemsworth."

"Sorry to interrupt the moment." He looked around. "Where's the kid?"

"With your cousin Enzo? There's a chess tournament in town for the next two nights. I cleared it with Luca before letting him go."

He cocked his head to the side. "Not as interesting as a date with Chris Evans."

"Hemsworth."

He waved his hand dismissively. "All Hollywood Chrises are interchangeable," he muttered. "I'll just get out of your way then. Are you good to leave at nine tomorrow for the hospital?"

"Do you want to join me?" Why the fuck was I asking that? Was it because of the longing I was seeing in his eyes? Or because of mine? I'd never had the house to myself with Domenico, and it made me giddy like a teen at her first make-out party.

Yes, but you're not a teen anymore, India, and this guy is not your crush...

"Do you think you'll have enough to share?" He pointed at my sixteen-ounce tub of ice cream.

"Obviously not!" I snorted. "You need to get your own." I turned around to walk in the living room, discreetly removing the spot patch once my back was to him. It was too late to do anything for my appearance now that he saw me.

"So, what are we watching?" he asked, joining me on the sofa, and I was pleased by the fact he sat right beside me and not on the other end.

"Action movie… Lots of violence, blood and shirtless scenes."

"Ah, yes, shirtless scenes are my favorites."

I chuckled, some of the remaining tension leaving me. Despite what he was and what he represented, I couldn't help but feel a kinship with him. I felt safe.

We were about twenty minutes into the film when I leaned into him.

I felt him tense and immediately regretted it. I started to move away when he caught me around the shoulders.

"No, don't move." The strain in his voice made me frown.

I disengaged myself and looked at him. He looked… frazzled.

"I'm sorry," he offered, looking away.

"Why are you—" I stopped as my eyes connected with his growing erection. "Oh!"

His obvious embarrassment dimmed some of my pleasure at having him react that way to me even in my most unkempt way.

"There's nothing to be sorry about. It's natural."

He shook his head. "My body doesn't usually react like that. You're unsettling me on so many levels."

His reaction to all of this really confused me. "You are not into sex?"

He sighed, resting his head on the back of the sofa, looking up at the ceiling. "No, I enjoy sex. It's just—" He stopped talking and I hated that he was not looking at me while he spoke. I wanted to look into his eyes.

"It's just that you usually react to men more than

women?" I tried to guess where his conflict was coming from. "There's nothing wrong with that."

He grimaced and shook his head again. "I know there's nothing wrong with that but no, I'm only attracted to women. Believe me."

"Dom, look at me, please."

He kept his head on the back of the sofa but turned toward me, throwing me a look full of uncertainty.

I reached for his hand and squeezed it. "What is it? Tell me."

He closed his eyes for a second and emitted another sigh full of weariness. When he opened them, I saw a pit of sadness and turmoil that made my heart ache.

"I'm not gentle," he started to say.

"You are gentle. I saw you with Cassie and Jude."

He shook his head. "No, I mean in bed. I'm not gentle and even just saying that is an understatement."

Ah, he liked it rough... not as rare as he might have thought it was.

"You cuddle against me. I feel your warm body against me and," He sat up straighter. "I don't usually respond to softness... Quite the contrary. I want the tears, the fear."

I was stung by his revelation but tried to keep my face as impassive as possible. He was looking at me, trying to see the disgust he expected and maybe even wanted to see there.

I knew what he was not saying; of course I did. He liked to role-play and not just any role, he craved non-con.

I nodded. "Why do you?"

He stood up briskly and turned around, pointing an accusing finger at me. "Don't start playing your psychologist crap on me. Don't try to be my doctor."

I stood up slowly, standing a few steps from him. "Lord, no, I don't want to be your doctor."

He gave me a small, snarky smile. "Too messed up?"

I shook my head. "No, because the feelings I have for you would be frowned upon by the board."

"What are you saying?"

The apprehension I felt now, as my heart started to hammer in my chest, felt the same as when I went base jumping and it was quite fitting, come to think of it. I was free jumping now on an emotional level and it was so much more terrifying.

"I'm a therapist, yes, but I'm a woman first." I took a deep breath. "A woman attracted to you in ways she'd never been to anyone else. A woman who came here to start fresh, take a break from anything with a penis and be herself and who fell right under the spell of Dom! A woman who is obsessed with you..." There, it was out.

He looked at me with a frown, his jaw set. He looked both offended and angry at my words.

"It's what you deserve for making me obsessed with you." His voice was lower, and despite the accusations in it, I could hear the heat. "For cracking my fucking chest open and seeping through the cracks of the little peace of mind I had left."

That was one way to admit our attraction to each other. It was weird and really backward, but I suspected a relationship between us would be like that.

He thought he was a lost cause—that much was clear—but that was not the case. His body had responded to me and there had been no roughness, no pain. He was not broken. He could find pleasure in other parts of sex; he just needed to know that.

I took a step toward him. "Do you trust me, Dom?"

He looked down at me, his dark eyes a pit of doubt. "I shouldn't."

"Not my question."

"I do, Lord knows I shouldn't, but I do."

I grabbed his hand and pulled him toward my bedroom. I was always overthinking everything and it never really worked out for me.

I felt a visceral attraction for Dom, almost felt it from the moment I met him, and he admitted feeling the same? I had to go with my gut for once and even if it didn't lead to anything, then what? I'd be leaving eventually.

"India, I can't," he said softly, but his actions contradicted his words as he followed me. "It won't work. Not the way I'd like for it to work."

Once we were in my room, I turned around and met his troubled eyes.

"I want you, Dom."

He took a sharp intake of breath. "That's not the problem, India. I—"

I rested my fingers against his lips to stop him. "Do you want me?" I asked, running my hand slowly down his muscular chest, hooking my finger on his leather belt.

"More than my next breath," he admitted, leaning down almost in spite of himself and barely brushing his soft lips against mine.

I pressed my lips against his, taking the leap and initiating the kiss we were both craving.

He brought his hand to the back of my head, deepening the kiss, his tongue dominating as he explored me in a consuming way. The rich alcohol taste of his mouth was almost as intoxicating as his kiss.

"Give me control," I whispered breathlessly against his lips once we broke the kiss.

He rested his forehead against mine, rubbing his nose against mine in an Eskimo kiss. "I never give up control."

"I know you don't, but do it for me—for us. We owe it to us to at least try." I jerked my head toward the headboard. "If you don't like it, we'll stop."

He threw me an uncertain look before looking at the bed again, and I could see right then and there he decided to take a chance on us.

I sighed with relief when he started to unbutton his dress shirt, keeping his dark soulful eyes trained on me. The intensity of his gaze made my lower stomach twist in a very pleasant way. How could a man manage to arouse me with just a look?

He discarded his shirt, and I couldn't help but study his chest, not caring about how in awe I must have looked. As expected he was muscular, with defined abs and the *V* by the hips that make smart girls like me extremely stupid. I let my eyes trail up to his well-developed pecs covered with a fine dust of dark hair and the single tattoo on the right side of it.

As if compelled I brought a shaky hand up and traced the tattoo gently, as if he would crumble under my touch.

He took a sharp intake of breath as I traced the dagger—the word 'Omerta' on top of it—and rested my forefinger on top of the cross at the end of the rosary.

Dom brought his hand up and rested it on top of mine.

I looked up and we just stared into each other's eyes. For how long? I was not sure. Time had lost any value to me. All that seemed to matter was his eyes on mine, his body heat, and his frantic heartbeat resonating in my hand.

"You are the brightest star in the darkest night," he whispered after a while before kissing me again.

"On the bed," I let out before I lost the resolve I had and begged him to take me now, just any way he'd like.

He let out a little growl of frustration but took a step back, breaking the trance, then he lay on the bed, his eyes still full of doubt of what was to come.

"You have to trust me," I said as I undid his belt and pulled it out of his pants.

"I do. It's me I don't trust with you."

I shook my head. "Give it a chance. Grab the headboard," and he did as I asked.

I tried to keep my face smooth as I tied the hands of this big powerful man. It was the first time I actually did something like that and knowing who he was, made it so much more erotic.

Once his hands were secure, I reached for his zipper and opened it slowly, letting the anticipation burn us both. I pulled his pants and briefs just enough to free his massive erection from its restraint. I couldn't help the little smile spreading across my lips, and the lustful glint in his eyes indicated he was satisfied with my reaction.

This man was all in proportion. I had my share of

partners in my life, but Domenico was clearly in a category of his own.

He rested his head against the pillow and let out a sound that seemed part moan and part growl as he thrusted his hips in the air. He wanted his release with my mouth around his cock, and the thought of bringing him pleasure aroused me to the point of discomfort.

I knelt on the floor and looked at his massive cock resting on his lower stomach.

"You don't have to," he said breathlessly, clearly mistakenly interpreting my assessment as doubt.

I grabbed his cock in my hand and squeezed a little. "I know I don't." I leaned closer, rolling my tongue across the head of his cock and licking away his precum. "But I really want to."

Meeting his eyes, I leaned down and kissed his lower stomach, getting closer and closer to where I knew he wanted me. He bucked his hips, and I licked his lower stomach. He wanted me to get on with it, but I also enjoyed the teasing, the tenderness, even in the heat of the moment.

He let out a loud moan mixed with a sigh when I pulled one of his balls into my mouth.

"India!" He sighed in pleasure. His stomach was taut, his hands in tight fists, his head thrown back in ecstasy. I'd never felt like this; I'd never wanted to give more pleasure to anyone in my life.

I removed his balls from my mouth and started

licking up his shaft. The tip of my tongue worked its way up the sensitive underside of his cock until it reached right under the ridge of his head.

"Please, just please," he begged, bucking his hips again.

I decided to stop the torturing pleasure and finally put my lips around the whole head of his cock and gently started to suck him.

He let out a sigh of relief as I started to fondle his balls with one hand and slowly lowered my mouth over his entire length, getting it deep inside and down my throat.

"Fuck, India!" he roared as I swallowed around his cock. "I could die now. I'd die a fucking happy man."

His words of praise aroused me even more, and I started to bob my head up and down with more fervor.

He began to buck his hips up and down, in sync with my bobbing motion. I stroked the root of his cock with my hands as I swallowed his shaft again.

Swirling my tongue around the underside of his head, I was riding my own pleasure at his reaction to my ministrations.

He bucked his hips faster, harder while groaning and moaning shamelessly, coming completely undone under my touch, letting go of all his guards and apprehension, becoming the raw, sexual man I had been eager to discover.

My suction became firmer with every downward

stroke, and I couldn't help but start to moan too, showing him that I enjoyed his undoing almost as much as he did.

I swished his cock inside my cheeks, getting it as deep into my throat as possible. His cock was completely inside my mouth as his groans turned louder, his breathing more erratic. I closed my eyes as I grabbed his dick with strong suctions while fondling his sack.

"India... I can't hold it much longer..." he let out pleadingly.

I didn't answer but sucked him faster and made moaning noises, preparing to finish him off.

"Fuck, India, baby, you're killing me."

His erection flexed as I focused my mouth and tongue intently on the head of his dick while tightening my grip around his balls.

His explosion came with a feral scream, and I bobbed my head up and down quickly, swallowing spurt after spurt of hot cum as it shot down my throat.

Completely spent and drained, he collapsed back on the bed as I lovingly stroked his thighs, his cock still in my mouth as his muscles visibly relaxed.

As I slowly withdrew, I gave the head of his cock a soft, little kiss, licking away the last remaining drops of his salty fluid.

I stood up and looked at him. He blinked a few times and gave me a side smile.

"Untie me. I need to touch you." His voice was gravelly with the force of his orgasm.

As soon as I unhooked the belt, he grabbed me around the waist much faster than a man his size should do, and I squealed with surprise when he pulled me toward him and twirled so I was lying on my back and he was hovering over me.

"Thank you," he rasped before giving me a chaste kiss. "That was… mind-blowing."

I brought my hand up, cradling his cheek. "You're most welcome. And see? You don't need to dominate to enjoy it."

"True." He pushed his leg between mine and pressed against my aching core. "But I prefer it that way."

I smiled up at him and raised my hips, looking for the friction to help ease my arousal. "And I won't stop you from dominating me. I can even say I'm looking forward to it, but I just wanted you to see that you can enjoy sex without it."

"It's a first," He traced my jawline with his lips. "This is you, India." He nibbled at my ear. "I just needed to find you."

His revelation left me speechless. How could he say things that went straight to my heart, awakening a desire so deep it hurt me?

"Now it's my turn to have fun," he announced before pulling my shirt up and taking my erect nipple in his mouth, gently sucking on it while his hand trailed down my stomach and disappeared into the waistband of my sweatpants, straight into my panties.

I moaned as his cool fingers rubbed against my wet, burning core.

He let go of my nipple with a pop as he kept on rubbing me up and down, pressing against my swollen clit with each passing.

"You're so wet." He kissed me passionately, dominating all of me with his tongue. "Did giving me a blow job excite you that much?"

I nodded, unable to speak.

"Um, my naughty girl," he cooed before grabbing my bottom lip between his teeth, biting hard enough to make me feel it but not enough to break the skin.

I gasped as one of his fingers entered me slowly. I opened my legs wider, raising my hips shamelessly, seeking more.

"Don't worry, beautiful. I'll give you what you need," he said, adding a second finger, filling me so deliciously.

I let my head fall against the pillow and closed my eyes, surrendering to the bliss of his fingers moving rhythmically inside of me while his thumb rubbed against my clit and his mouth latched at my breasts like a starving man at a buffet.

I slid my fingers into his coarse black hair and raised my hips rhythmically with the back and forth of his fingers.

And suddenly as he curled his fingers inside of me, touching my G-spot, I tightened my hand in his hair as my orgasm took me under, like a tidal wave submerging me in a sea of pleasure so intense it was almost painful.

I came, shouting his name, not caring that I could probably be heard from the other side of the world. It was the best orgasm I ever had, and he'd given it to me with just his fingers and tongue.

I took a couple of deep breaths as he rested a protective hand on my stomach, brushing his lips against my cheekbone.

"You are absolutely beautiful but with this post orgasmic glow? You are mesmerizing."

I gave him a small, tired smile. I was way too satisfied and relaxed to say anything.

He lay back down and pulled me to him, my chest resting against his strong, warm chest.

I closed my eyes, listening to the tranquil beating of his heart, feeling his gentle caress on my lower back, and as I relaxed, I fell asleep.

10

DOM

After she fell asleep on my chest, I looked at her for a few minutes. Her beautiful plump lips, swollen by our passionate kissing, were slightly open. I took in her graceful straight nose and her long black eyelashes. This girl couldn't be real; no woman could be that beautiful, patient, and kindhearted. I could not be that lucky... I didn't deserve to be that lucky, and yet here she was, tangible, her slim body pressed against mine, the swell of her breast against my chest.

I sighed as I reluctantly slid out of the bed. The kid would be back soon, and I didn't want to wake her up.

I took a quick shower, put on some loose sweatpants, and waited for the kid while eating some Chinese leftovers from the night before.

I could hardly believe how relaxed and satisfied I really felt. I didn't think I ever felt that way.

Every time I was satisfying my sexual needs, I felt ashamed afterward. I hated the monster that came out every time I had to satisfy my needs. I truly hated that part of me, but this time the monster didn't come out. I enjoyed her mouth, her tongue... I enjoyed making her come so hard I was sure she'd passed out for a few seconds. I loved it and I didn't feel like a monster... I felt like a man, and it was all thanks to her.

Once the kid was back and tucked away in his bedroom, I should have gone back to my bedroom, but instead I went back to hers where she was still peacefully asleep. I was not ready for our moment to end, not after the physical and emotional connection we just shared and especially since I was unsure if there would be a tomorrow for us, if she'd still wanted us in the morning. If she did, we would have to talk, set ground rules because dating me was bound to be hard on her and I was not certain I was worth the effort.

I sighed, shaking my head. It was not the time to let my thoughts turn dark and get the best of me. I just had to enjoy my time with her a little more. So I joined her in bed, spooning her and I felt like a superhero when she nestled against me, letting out a little sigh of comfort. I did that to her.

I buried my face in her soft curls that held a faint smell of jasmine, and I fell asleep, feeling at peace for the first time in years.

When I woke up the next morning, I didn't dare move as we'd shifted position during the night and she was now half on top of me, her face buried in my neck, her arm around my torso, and her long, slender leg between mine, her thigh pressing against my growing erection.

I turned my head to look at the clock and groaned. *Eight a.m.!* I couldn't remember the last time I actually slept past five a.m. Maybe it was because I hated being asleep and only tried to sleep the bare minimum I needed to survive.

I hated sleep because it was the only time I could not try to control my thoughts and the nightmares hit so hard sometimes, bringing back the horror I'd done, the horrors I'd witnessed helplessly... I woke up some mornings with the vivid memories of these girls' scared eyes and a fresh new coat of self-hatred.

But I had no dream last night and woke up feeling almost normal. I idly traced her spine with my fingers, trying to wake her up as gently as possible.

She let out a little moan and moved her leg, hardening my cock to the point of pain.

"Just five minutes," she mumbled against my neck.

I let out a little laugh, resting my hand possessively on her ass. I wanted to stay in bed with her but the way my body reacted? I was not sure I could resist, and we were expected to go to the hospital in an hour.

"You stay in bed. I'll get up and make breakfast." I kissed her forehead.

Disentangling myself from her body was the hardest thing I ever had to do, but duty and Luca came first... at least right now.

I threw her a last look as she turned around on the bed. I sighed. This woman was more addictive than any drug.

When I went to my room across the hall, I noticed that the kid was already in the kitchen area eating a bowl of cereal, watching some show about chess—his newfound obsession.

I took a quick shower, shaved, and trimmed my goatee before settling on my dark-gray suit and purple shirt. I'd seen how her eyes lit up when I wore that damn shirt, and I was half tempted to buy twenty more just for her to look at me like that every day.

You got it bad, man. I could hear Luca's voice in my head. That was karma returning the favor for mocking him for his obsession with Cassie.

I stopped by her bedroom on my way to the kitchen, but she was not in bed anymore and I could hear the faint sound of the shower from the bathroom.

"Is India your girlfriend?" Jude asked as soon as I walked in the main room.

Fuck me! I winced as I walked into the kitchen and started to put out bowls and the different types of cereal, hoping I could pretend I didn't hear him and he'd go back to watching his show.

I let out a breath when he didn't talk again. I'd dodged a bullet there. What could I even tell him? What was last night? Was it just a slipup? A way to satisfy the attraction? I didn't know if it worked for her, but that one backfired on me because if I was obsessed before... I was completely consumed now.

I turned on the coffee maker and spun around to see a pair of green eyes and a mop of light-brown hair looking at me critically.

"Holy fuck!" I took a step back.

Jude was kneeling on one of the bar stools, his hands resting on the breakfast bar.

"You shouldn't swear; it's not nice," he chastised me with a little shake of his head.

"That's true. You just took me by surprise. You were there." I pointed in the corner by the flat screen TV. "I turn around and you appear right here, like a mini ninja."

Jude grinned, showing his cute gap between his front teeth. He enjoyed taking me by surprise.

"I asked you a question, but you didn't hear me. Is India your girlfriend?"

"India?" I cleared my throat. I should have known

better. The kid had a one-track mind; he never dropped anything. "I, um, why are you asking?"

"The guys at school say if a boy sleeps in the same room as a girl, they are together."

"I see." Fuck, I hated his boarding school right about now.

"And I saw you go into her room last night, so is India your girlfriend?"

"Listen, buddy. Things are not as s—"

"I was so sure Solkiev would win the game last night. I guess Johnson was just lucky," India interrupted.

The kid turned to her, his mouth opened wide with outrage.

"This is not true! Johnson was way better!" He jumped from the stool. "I'll show you!" he called, running past her to his bedroom.

I threw her a grateful look that she met with a cheeky smile and a wink.

"I was promised breakfast," she said, crossing her arms on her chest.

Before Cassie, all the women I'd been surrounded by were always overly made up, perfect clothes, perfect hair, perfect makeup... so perfectly fake. That had been the role of most women in the famiglia. Their primary role was to look good for their husband, father, brother or whichever male family member they were with that day, but then Cassie entered our life and now this stunning woman.

She was dressed in a pair of black skinny jeans, with a long-sleeve red shirt and matching flats, and just like that, with her golden skin devoid of makeup, she was a thousand times more beautiful and enticing than any other woman in the famiglia.

I cleared my throat under the weight of emotions and gestured to the four boxes of cereal and the carton of milk on the counter.

"Oh." She nodded, walking to the counter and taking a seat. "This is the type of breakfast last night warranted? Fine, I'll just have to step up my game next time."

At that moment, the kid rushed back with a pile of magazines. I didn't even care that he interrupted. I was just grateful there would be a next time for us. I felt like I was floating on a cloud, my heart so full, it felt constricted in my chest.

Is this what falling in love feels like? I asked myself as I leaned on the counter, looking at her eating her cereal as she listened to Jude talk about the chess players from last night.

I drank my coffee silently, just looking at her and not fighting hot I felt, gladly drowning in my feelings for her.

Soon enough she was done with her breakfast and the cleaning lady came in.

We drove to the hospital, mostly chitchatting about the chess game Jude was going to see tonight.

"Thank you for before," I told her when we

entered the hospital and Jude ran ahead of us, much too excited to see his sister and his new nephew and niece.

She waved her hand dismissively. "It was a little early for that conversation."

I nodded silently as we waited for the elevator. It was too early, of course it was, and yet why was I ready to make a commitment? Because she was an enchanting goddess; it was the only possible explanation.

She reached for my hand and brushed her fingers against my palm. I closed my hand, not ready to let go. We stood side by side in the elevator, holding hands, and only let go when the doors opened on Cassie's floor.

The door was ajar, the kid already in the room and sitting on a chair by the bed, looking on in awe at his sister holding his brand-new niece.

"You made it." Luca chuckled, holding his infant son in his arms.

My heart squeezed in my chest at the look of pure happiness and tranquility on his face. It was all I'd ever wanted for my best friend. He deserved love and happiness, and after the car accident, I feared he would never get that, but now he had Cassie and his children.

Emotions clogged at my throat, making it hard to swallow.

I cleared my throat and turned to Cassie. "How

are you, baby mama?" I asked her with a little grin, going to the bed and giving her a kiss on her forehead before looking at the little girl in her arms.

She was so little, so fragile, a wave of protectiveness came over me. Something so powerful it almost knocked me down, and I swore right then and there I'd protect these children with my life.

"What a beautiful little princess," I murmured, not trusting my own voice under the overload of emotion that had been hitting me for the past few minutes.

I touched the little girl's button nose. "At least she doesn't have her father's nose, something to be grateful about."

"*Vaffanculo stronzo,*" Luca muttered, making me chuckle.

I turned my head toward him and winked.

He rolled his eyes, rocking the baby in his arms. "Domenico, don't you want to meet your godson?"

I froze. No, that was just too much. I looked away and blinked. Fuck it, I could feel the tears burning in my eyes.

I cleared my throat again. "There must be dust around here; my allergies are acting up."

"Probably," Cassie agreed as India, who was standing beside her, nodded her head in agreement.

"There's no dust here, and you don't have a dust allergy, Dom. Do you remember when we went in the attic?" Jude piped in.

We all laughed at his adorable obliviousness, easing some of the tension.

I walked to Luca who was standing at the end of the luxury hospital room and looked at the little boy he was holding, the heir to the Montanari legacy... How could such a small thing have such a heavy load on his shoulders?

"Meet Marco Domenico Montanari," Luca announced with so much pride.

"Domenico?" I asked in disbelief.

"The name of his godfather," Cassie announced from behind me.

I turned around to see the baby was now in India's arms. Lord, that woman appealed to all my primal needs.

I shook my head, shutting down where my thoughts and feelings were going. It was clearly not the time and place.

"And this is Arabella Maria," Cassie continued, throwing a dreamy look toward her daughter.

I nodded. "That's a wonderful name." Naming their little girl after Luca's late sister and mother was the best ode to them.

I turned back toward Luca and looked down at Marco. "I fear this one may have your nose though." I looked up with a smirk.

Luca rolled his eyes before extending his arms toward me.

"What are you doing?" I asked, raising my hand in a stop motion. Did my voice carry the panic I felt?

He laughed and shook his head. "Don't you want to hold him?"

I looked down at the tiny baby in his arms. "No, of course not. I will break him."

"You won't. Babies are more resistant than you think."

"Are those your words or your wife's?"

Luca threw a quick look toward Cassie. "What do you think?"

"Hers."

"Obviously!" He extended his arms a bit further. "I was even scared to touch them yesterday. It took a lot of pep talk, I admit, but once I had Marco and Arabella in my arms... I didn't want to let them go." He took a deep breath. "Just fold your arm like that."

I mimicked his position and stopped breathing as he set the baby in my arms, his neck secured in the crook of my elbow.

"Just keep his neck like that; it'll be fine."

When Luca let go, I exhaled a little whoosh of air, looking down at the dozing infant in my arms. He was there, right in my arms. Fuck, did I love these children already.

"I'm going to be the best godfather and uncle you'll ever get, kid." I looked up and met Cassie's eyes.

She was looking at me with a small smile, her

hand on her heart and her eyes full of love and tenderness.

I winked at her before quickly looking at India who was rocking Arabella. She gave me a small smile that seemed to say 'you got this,' and I felt my heart swell even more with her faith in me.

I turned back to Luca. "How does it feel? To be a father."

He looked away thoughtfully for a minute before turning toward me. "I am not sure I can really express how it feels. I thought I was ready. I didn't expect to feel the way I felt when I saw them. They got Marco out first and when I heard his first cry, my heart…" He rubbed at his chest. "It was instant love, a love so deep I almost fell on my knees. It was everything all at once, and if I thought I loved my wife before—" He shook his head. "It seems like a distant memory with the way I feel for her now, how I look at her every time she is nursing one of our babies." He looked up at the ceiling, his Adam's apple bobbing under the weight of his emotion. "I'd die without them. I'll gladly fall in the pit of hell with a fucking smile on my face if I lost them."

I looked down at Marco again before glancing toward Cassie who was chatting excitedly with India and Jude, somehow oblivious at the intense sharing of emotions and fear happening on this side of the room.

I met my best friend's eyes and saw the fear he was trying to hide.

"Nothing will happen to them. I'm here too. I'll protect your family with my life."

Luca rested his hand on the side of my neck. "Our family, fratello."

"Yea, our family."

Luca sighed, motioning us to the end of the room which had chairs. "Let's go sit for a while and talk."

I nodded, walking slowly so as not to wake up the baby in my arms and sat as carefully as possible, letting out a sigh of relief once my ass touched the seat.

"You seem okay." Luca started studying me critically. "I thought you'd be irritated after yesterday's dead end and going to Baker's Place." He grimaced. "All that for nothing."

I let out a short laugh. "I know. I took a shower with bleach when I came back just to make sure. Am I frustrated?" I shrugged. "Maybe a little. I'm more concerned than frustrated, and Matteo was frustrated enough for the both of us." I still hardly believed that I'd witnessed Matteo Genovese completely lose his cool.

Luca nodded, resting his hand on the armrest, tapping his forefinger rhythmically. "He called me last night."

I frowned. Couldn't Genovese just cut him a fucking break? He just became a father. How cold could that man be? "Whatever he asked you to do, tell me. I'll take care of it."

Luca gave me a small smile. "He didn't ask anything actually. He just wanted to know how Cassie and the babies were doing."

I raised my eyebrows, surprised that Matteo would ever show a modicum of concern for Luca and his family.

"I know. I was surprised too." He shook his head. "He just asked if you already told me about Baker's Place and that I should enjoy the time with my family that, and I quote, the 'knock-off capo' is more adequate than he anticipated and that you would do for the moment."

I let out a little snort. "I see… 'More adequate.' What a compliment."

"From Genovese, I think it is. The guy likes you, it seems."

"Genovese likes no one."

Luca shrugged. "I'm not convinced of that. It may be because I just became a father and the fatherly wisdom just fell upon me."

"I don't think that's how it works."

Luca waved his hand dismissively. "It totally does. I do think that Matteo Genovese feels much more than he leads us to believe."

I thought about his breakdown again. "Maybe…"

"What about you though? I saw the little bounce in your step. You seem at peace."

"I had sex," I whispered. Somehow it felt wrong to say that in a room with newborns.

Luca let out a little chuckle. "Good for you? I expected that much, being so close to The Rectory, and not using it would be a waste of an opportunity."

I shook my head. I couldn't lie to my best friend. "It was not The Rectory. I went there but I couldn't. There was only one woman I wanted." My eyes connected with India who was holding Arabella with a goofy smile on her face.

"I see." Luca's voice carried wariness. I couldn't blame him for it. It had the potential to get messy. "I didn't think India enjoyed…" He trailed off.

"I didn't need to do *that*."

Luca threw me a surprised look. "You didn't?"

I shook my head. "I gave her full control." I looked down at the baby sleeping in my arms, a little uncomfortable. "She bound my hands and I wanted her enough to try," I admitted.

"Uh," Luca looked at the two women again and nodded. "I'm happy for you."

"It doesn't mean anything," I replied quickly, somehow not wanting to nourish a hope that should not be there. It was too new, too fragile; who said I would not revert to the monster I was when my hands would be free?

Who said she even wanted more from this scary life full of rules, codes, and death?

"It should mean something. You know, you and

her, it's not impossible," he said as if he could read my thoughts. He jerked his head toward his wife. "Look at me and Cassie. I never thought a woman who was raised out of the famiglia could understand, could be the support needed, and yet Cassie is all of that and even more." He smiled dreamily at her, and as if she could feel it, she looked up. As their eyes met and she returned his smile, it was like two souls becoming one. Fuck, did I crave that.

"How?"

"As long as she understands that due to your line of work, the famiglia will often have to come first despite everything you feel for her. That putting the famiglia first will be crucial for your safety but that when the choice is truly yours, she will always come first, and sometimes you can just disconnect and be there *only* for her." He met my eyes. "And I'm lucky because I have you to rely on when I need to do that. I can leave it all behind and concentrate only on my wife because I know you are here to pick up where I left off."

"I'll always have your back."

"I know and I'll always have yours. You can do it too. Give this a shot, Dom. What do you have to lose?"

The piece of my heart that I thought was dead, I thought as icy fear lodged in my throat at the mere thought of India leaving.

His eyes softened and I knew he understood. "Think about all the things you could win."

"And knowing me, you're okay with that?" *Knowing what I did, what I could do?*

"Why wouldn't I be? The woman is a lucky one to have succeeded where many have failed; she stole Domenico's heart."

I narrowed my eyes with suspicion. Lucky? He thought she was lucky? It was much more a curse than a gift... She owned the tattered heart of a man who was also partially a monster. A monster lurking in his blood, ready to pounce at any moment... Yeah, that was shit luck right there.

"I know what I'm saying, Dom, and you won't convince me otherwise. I'm a tad annoyed though," he added with a playful sigh.

"Why?"

"I now owe my wife a hundred dollars."

"I don't get it."

He shook his head. "Last week she bet me you were going to hook up before the end of the month."

I looked at him, my mouth hanging open with surprise. Had I been so obvious? "You guys were gossiping about us like old ladies?"

"Maybe. You know at night in bed, my wife was much too pregnant for us to have fun so..."

"You're an asshole," I muttered, and at that moment, baby Marco started screaming his head off.

169

"Somebody's hungry." Luca laughed, grabbing the baby from me.

I stood up once I was free and shook my arm which was numb after holding the baby.

"What do you guys say we go grab lunch?" I asked India and Jude. "What would you like?" I asked Cassie and Luca, who gratefully gave us an order.

As we walked down the corridor to the elevator, I mustered all of my courage and grabbed India's hand.

She looked down with surprise but didn't remove it, and I felt my heart flutter in my chest. Was I morphing into a teenage girl?

"Let me take you out for dinner tonight. What do you say? Just the two of us?"

She grinned at me with a small nod. "It's a date."

Thank fuck for that! "Yes, it is."

11

DOM

A date. I wasn't completely sure why I asked or why she agreed, but I was having second thoughts. Not about her, no. Nothing as good as India was supposed to be in my life, and I knew full well that she was just as good as I could ever get.

I was worried for her, about what being with me entailed. Mafia men were not better than old yentas, and if we were seen together in town, the rumor mill would be going full force, and she would be associated with me no matter what she did.

I took a quick shower and changed into a pair of black pants and a light-blue dress shirt.

I looked at myself in the mirror as I styled my

hair, feeling lighter than I had in a long time despite what was at stake here.

My phone vibrated, indicating a text. I closed my eyes for a second before looking at it. I was just so close to getting a lovely evening with a stunning woman, an evening during which I could almost feel normal, and I wanted it to last just a few seconds more. I should have known better than to expect a break. Karma was a fucking bitch and my life was supposed to be a long penance for what I did, what I witnessed, what I didn't stop.

Here goes nothing. I reached for my phone on the dresser and opened the text from an unknown number.

I'm watching you.

My nostrils flared. That was the fucking bastard that left notes on my car; he was stepping up his game now. How did he even get my number?

Why just watch? Come closer and suck my dick, I typed back. I'd die before he thought he was scaring me. Was he annoying me? Definitely. But scared? No. Rare were the things that could scare me now.

I waited a couple of minutes and flipped my middle finger to the phone. That shut the fucker up.

I straightened my shirt, adjusted my belt, and looked at myself once more in the mirror.

I've never been vain; appearance didn't matter that much to me. I knew women liked me, at least how I looked—if they knew the monster lurking so close to the surface, they'd run...

I opened the door and any dark thoughts or doubts just vanished instantly at the view of the goddess in front of me.

She had her black hair in a plait that went over her right shoulder, dressed in a simple green, flowy knee-length dress. The dress almost matched her eyes and it complemented her skin in ways that made it so hard for me to keep my hands to myself. The only little extra on her was her pink lipstick and her big hoop earrings. It was all so simple; nothing extra but she didn't need anything. I'd seen that woman bare, and she didn't need anything to bring me to my knees.

Fuck! My dick twitched again. Now was not the time to think of India naked.

I cleared my throat and looked down, picturing the death scene from Baker's Place, hoping to put my dick into a coma for the next few hours.

"I, um, I can change if it's not suitable. Sorry. I was not sure the evening you'd—"

I grabbed her face in my hands as gently as possible and leaned down, brushing my lips against hers softly, and I had to stop myself from deepening the kiss.

"Don't ever doubt yourself, *Dolcetta.* You're breathtaking no matter what you wear." I brushed my nose against her.

"You just stood there, in silence," she said with an uncertainty that disconcerted me. How could she be insecure?

"I just had to catch my breath after seeing you, is all. You do that to me."

"What?"

"Take all the air out of my lungs."

She smiled brightly at me and once again, seeing her looking at me like I was a hero made me feel a little like one.

I let go of her face and extended my arm to her with a playful smile. "Ready to go, beautiful?"

"Sure." She took my arm without hesitation, causing my heart to tighten once more in my chest.

Did Luca feel like that too when he was with Cassie? No wonder he was addicted.

"Where are we going?" she asked when we finally sat in the car.

"The best steakhouse in town." Thanks to Luca's ownership of the place, we had a table whenever we wanted.

After a five-minute drive, I stopped in front of the restaurant and quickly exited and rounded the car to help India out.

"You didn't have to," she said, taking my hand.

"Of course I did," I replied, intertwining our fingers together. "It's a first date."

She shook her head but the bright smile she gave me was the perfect answer. She loved the attention.

Was it not something she was used to? I expected a woman like her to be lavished with attention, and yet every small gesture from me seemed like everything.

I threw my key to the valet. "Don't park it too far."

He bowed his head. "Of course. I will take great care of it."

As soon as we walked in, the blond hostess smiled brightly before letting her eyes rake down my arm to my hand holding India's, her face looking a little dejected before being replaced by her usual generic smile.

"Mr. Romano, what a pleasure to see you tonight."

"Thank you." I looked around and noticed a couple of men from the famiglia sitting at the bar and looking at us unabashedly.

Yep, everybody will know about my attachment before the food hits the table.

I turned back to India and the happy light in her eyes made it all worth it.

"Will anybody else be joining you this evening?" the hostess asked, resting her hand on the burgundy-colored menus I knew by heart.

I raised India's hand up and kissed the back of it. "No, it's only us."

The hostess let out a little sigh at the same time as India and I had to do my best to stop from grinning at their reactions.

"Very well." The hostess grabbed two menus and

gestured for us to follow her to the back of the restaurant.

We loved our privacy in the famiglia, especially with what happened to Luca's father and how he'd been gunned down in a restaurant. Now we made sure to sit as far as possible from the windows.

"This place looks amazing," India said in awe as we sat in the booth, hiding us from unwanted eyes or ears. This was useful when we were discussing deals that needed to be done in public, but I was more than grateful tonight to be in my bubble with India.

"It does," I agreed, reluctantly letting her go of her hand to allow her to look at the menu.

"Do you come here often?" she asked curiously as she scanned the menu.

"I used to. Luca owns it."

She looked at me with wide eyes. "He does?"

I laughed and nodded. "Yes, I even helped him figure out the menu."

"Wow…" She looked down at her menu before closing it and resting her hands on top of it. "Since you're basically the expert, pick something for me."

"Okay." I once again felt the warmth in my chest at the trust she put in me, even if it was a trivial one. "Anything you don't like?"

"No, just pick."

Once the waitress came, I ordered two ossobuco and some Dolcetto wine.

After we ordered she leaned closer and reached for my hand.

"Why are you looking at me like that?" She cocked her head to the side.

I leaned back on my chair. "Like what?"

"Like you expect me to bolt any minute."

"Ah." She was perceptive, and I didn't know if it was due to her field of work or our connection. "I wonder when will be the point I'll say or do something that will make you run in the other direction."

"I won't."

I nodded, then grabbed my glass of wine and took a sip. "We investigated you before letting you come," I admitted. "You don't seem surprised."

She shook her head a little, grabbing her glass of wine too. "I'm not. Knowing your line of work? I could not expect otherwise."

"I think it's only fair for me to start sharing as well."

"Only if you want to."

"You know most of us have nicknames. Luca was the Broken Prince. Matteo is the Cruel King."

"Very fitting."

"Do you want to know what they call me?"

She looked at me silently, inviting me to continue.

I took a deep breath, apprehension growing exponentially. Sharing with her was risky but I had to. If we even had a small chance to build something, she had to know some of my darkness.

"They are calling me Twisted Knight."

"Okay." She rested her glass back on the table and locked her all-knowing emerald eyes on me. "You know, I'm not saying or thinking your hands are clean, Dom. I am not as naïve as it seems. You've clearly suffered and gone through trauma. I'm not fooling myself thinking you're a saint. I even suspect what might be what caused this self-hatred but I'm not here to make you talk about what you don't want to talk about, what you are not ready to share." She reached across the table and interlinked our fingers together. "And if you're never ready to share, it's okay too."

I blinked a couple of times, not even sure she was real. Did she really suspect what I'd done and still held my hand?

"You asked me about Jake," she said softly, letting go of my hand as the waitress brought our food.

"You don't have to," I said, even if I was dying to find out more about that man that I hated on principle.

She took a deep breath. "I have a tendency to pick men with issues."

I let out a low chuckle as I cut my veal. "I can confirm, you don't know what you signed for when you picked me."

She cocked her head. "I think I do."

"I'm bad." How many times would I need to say it

for her to walk away? I may not be strong enough to let her go, but she had to be smarter than me.

She shook her head. "Not deep down and that's the main difference between them and you. They were all bright and light outside but so... ugly inside, but you are darkness on the outside, but I saw all the light—in your tender gestures toward Cassie, in your concern for me, in your patience and kindness with Jude. You're trying to smother it, but it's there. You're not a bad man."

I looked down at my nose, my nostrils flaring, already getting angry at what was to come.

"A real bad man doesn't think he is bad," she continued. "I came to help Cassie with her pregnancy and the babies, but I was happy to leave for a while." She kept her eyes down, running her peach-painted forefinger nail back and forth on the while table-cloth. "I met him a couple of years ago. He's an archi-tect. On paper he was perfect, but it was on paper only." She brought her hand to her face, brushing the beautiful velvet skin under her eye.

I wanted to murder that man for touching her in any way that was not consensual, touching her in any way that hurt her.

"India, look at me... Please," I added as my request sounded too much like an order.

She looked up, her emerald eyes glistening under the light. That man had to die for her distress.

"You are amazing, strong, kind. You're the most amazing woman I've ever met."

"But I'm also the woman who ran past all the red flags, the woman who let a man hit her, using all the same excuses she'd seen her patients use time and time again." She sighed. "I'm not just one thing. I can be brave and fall too. Same goes for you."

"I want to kill him."

"There's no need to go around plotting his murder."

"Oh, I don't need 'plotting.' I've got it all figured out."

She laughed, as if I was joking. Little did she know I'd never been more serious in my life. I had plans A to Z already in my repertoire and a call to the West Coast Canadian consigliere of the famiglia… and Jake 'the girlfriend-beater' will be nothing but a distant memory.

"Some part of me is grateful to him."

I couldn't help but frown in disbelief… That was certainly not something I expected.

She let out a soft melodious laugh. "Don't worry. I'm not crazy, but as you know, I've been raised by a scatter-brained mother who lived her dreams despite bills and other social restraint. I've been too used to worrying, and I grew up so serious, never taking any risk, always picking the safest, most sensible choice." She shook her head slightly. "If things with Jake didn't happen, I don't think I would have just jumped on a plane here, to a place I'd never been before, and I would have never met you and that would have been a shame." She looked away, her cheeks tainted with embarrassment.

My heart squeezed in my chest. How could she think so highly of me? "I'm not sure I'm worth any hardship."

"I do."

I wanted to grab her and kiss her senseless right here, at that table.

I shook my head. "You're something else."

"Is it a compliment?"

"The best there is."

Her smile widened. "I'll take it."

"Dessert?" the waitress asked once we were done with our meal.

I looked at India. "If you want a dessert, you should try the tiramisu. It's amazing."

She shook her head. "No, I think I'm ready to go home."

"Oh, okay." I tried to hide my disappointment at her wish to finish our evening early. Did I misinterpret the signs? I was not an expert. Truth be told, it was actually my first date ever but still, I was certain it was going well.

I nodded once more, reaching for my wallet inside my jacket.

The waitress shook her head. "No, Mr. Romano.

Your money is not good here. You have a great evening."

After she left the table, I still reached for my wallet and got out two twenties for the waitress.

"Dom, I had a great time," India said gently.

I nodded again, not sure what to reply. The fact that she was trying to spare my feelings made it somehow worse.

"I'm just ready for us to go home and continue what we started last night."

I looked up quickly, meeting her eyes with incredulity.

She laughed at my sudden interest. "Why did you think I wanted to leave?" She gave me a seductive smile that went straight to my cock. "I want dessert, but what I want is not on the menu."

I growled, looking heavenward. "You're killing me, woman. I'm now going to walk out with a tent in my pants."

She giggled. "And I'm okay with that."

I stood up quickly and reached for her hand to help her up.

"We need to move now, Dolcetta, or my hard-on will poke someone in the wrong place."

She laughed again and took my hand. "We wouldn't want that, would we?"

Fuck, I was addicted to her melodic laugh. I wanted to hear it every day... Well, that and her moans of pleasure, and I wanted to be the one creating all of these sounds. Maybe because her laugh, giving her pleasure, made me feel like I was invincible.

We exited the restaurant and my phone vibrated in my pocket as we were waiting for the car to be pulled around.

I opened the text without even looking at the sender. *'How does she feel about having dinner facing a rapist? Does she know the extent of your sins? Have you confessed your crimes?'*

I tightened my hold around my phone as I looked around, ready to murder anyone holding a phone in my vicinity.

"Dom?"

I looked down at her, my scowl still firmly in place.

Her eyes widened with worry, and I tried my best to smooth my features; she didn't deserve it.

She looked down at my hand holding the phone. "Is everything okay?"

That was what that coward wanted, to ruin my perfect evening with this amazing woman. He wouldn't have texted just now if it was not the case. I wouldn't give him satisfaction. I deserve some happiness too, and if this woman was kind enough to see past all the darkness in me and my life, then I would not let him take that away from me.

"Yes, sorry. Something at work that annoyed me."

"Oh, okay." She bit her plump bottom lip. "You can go if you want. I understand completely."

I shook my head and grabbed her hand as the valet parked the car in front of us.

"Nope, tonight is our night."

We drove back to the condo and the closer we got, the more I felt the tension build in the car, to the point that my dick already started to swell in my pants.

That was also new to me, getting hard just at the anticipation to be in this woman.

I glanced toward her and noticed how tightly she pressed her thighs together, how she moved a little from side to side, seeking friction.

My dick hardened a little more knowing she was probably already soaking wet for me.

I could almost smell her arousal, and I could so perfectly picture it, her pretty pussy, slick with her need for me, her lips swollen with desire. I let out an audible growl as my dick pressed painfully against the zipper of my pants.

I was already out of my head with need for her. I had to remain in control. I could not unleash the beast on her.

She mattered to me; I couldn't lose her.

We got out of the car, and she looked down at the bulge in my pants as we got into the elevator.

She walked to me and started to kiss me softly. I

pulled her toward me, pressing my erection on her lower belly.

I grabbed her plump bottom lip between my teeth and bit, not hard enough to draw blood but enough to make her gasp.

I invaded her mouth, tasting her. I grabbed the back of her head, holding her hair in a tight fist, kissing her as if my life depended on it.

When the elevator beeped, I pulled her into the condo without breaking the kiss. I didn't think I could if I wanted to; she was my opium.

I finally broke the kiss when my lungs started to scream for air.

"Is it possible to come with just a kiss?" she asked, looking at me with unfocused eyes, her pupils dilated so much she looked high, and she was high with the same desire I had for her.

She let her hands trail down my shirt to my leather belt.

I grabbed her wrists to stop her. "I want you so much, but I'm scared to hurt you." Especially now, especially knowing that she had been abused before. I wasn't sure I could control the beast.

I knew with her it was different. Usually, my dick only reacted to tears, begging, and fear. With her it just reacted; it wanted her all the time. Fear was not necessary, but there was a roughness in me, no matter how much I wanted to be gentle, and I wasn't sure it was a part of me I could control in the heat of the moment. Fuck, I could barely control the beast now.

All I wanted to do was grab her by the hair, twirl her around, and bend her over the table before fucking her raw, like an animal until I came in her and over her, marking her like the caveman I truly was.

She pulled at my hold on her wrists. "I'm not a broken doll, Domenico," she snapped before pursing her lips.

Oh... she was using my full name; I was walking a thin line here.

"No, Dolcetta, I-"

"Don't make me regret talking to you."

I grabbed her hand and kissed her palm. "I would never, but I want you so much. I don't think I can control myself."

She licked her lips slowly, keeping her sultry eyes on me. "Then don't. Give me the beast, Dom. I can take it," she assured, resting her hand on my bulge and squeezing.

"India..." I warned her.

"Show me the beast, Domenico."

She'd done it; she unleashed him.

"You asked for it." I pointed at the table. "Bend over and wait for me," I commanded.

She pressed her legs together, biting the corner of her bottom lip. Could she actually enjoy it? I prayed to every god willing to listen that she did.

She walked silently to the wooden table and leaned on it, tilting her head to the side to look at me.

I kept my eyes on her as I undid my belt and removed it through the hoops of my pants and wrapped it very slowly around my fist.

I walked a little closer to her as I opened my pants, bringing them and my underwear down just enough to free my hard steel cock.

She licked her lips again, rubbing her legs together.

"You want my ten inches, don't you, Dolcetta?"

She nodded against the table, licking her lips once again. I was pretty sure she was replaying the blow job she gave me yesterday, how she made herself choke on my cock.

I closed my eyes, taking a deep breath. If I keep thinking about that, I'll come before entering her, and that would be the worst crime.

"Put your wrists together on the table ahead of you."

She did as she was asked, completely submitting to my demands. It had to be a dream; I could not be this lucky.

I leaned over her, resting my cock on her backside. She was not just wet; she was positively soaked, her arousal seeping through her panties wetting my balls. Oh, she was more than ready for me.

I pressed my chest against her back, making her feel my weight, my power as I wrapped the belt tightly around her wrist, keeping one end in my hand.

I thrust my hips forward a couple of times, mimicking sex as my cock rubbed between our bodies.

She let out a little mewl of want.

"Tell me what you want, Dolcetta," I whispered against her ear, as I thrust.

"You... Please, Dom, I want you," she begged.

"Me? What part of me?"

She let out a moan.

I thrust again. "Answer the question, India; which part of me do you want?"

"Your cock, deep inside of me," she replied in a breath.

I kept my chest on her back but moved my hips just enough to pull up her dress and pull down her panties.

I nudged her foot to spread her legs a little wider and stood up, pulling the belt with me, forcing her to arch her back as her arms were pulled back.

I ran my hand on the curve of her ass, the dip of her hips. She shivered under my touch.

I brought my hand forward, running my fingers between her heated wet folds.

I grabbed the condom from my back pocket and opened it with my teeth, my hands shaking with desire as I rolled it on my painful cock.

She let out a whimper as I entered her with my

forefinger; she was so warm and ready my finger slid right in. I added a second finger, and she tensed her inner muscle, trying to pull me deeper inside her.

"You're so ready for me."

She let out an incoherent noise that sounded like a moan and a plea.

I removed my fingers, placed my aching cock at her entrance, and I entered her in one forceful thrust while pulling hard on the belt, forcing her torso off the table as I impaled myself in her, all softness and tenderness flying out the window.

All I could hear was the caveman in me shouting I needed to possess this woman, claim her like she's mine in every way possible.

And if I believed the shout of pleasurable pain she let out when my cock forced its way down her tight channel, she wanted that too.

"Fuck, India!" I shouted, letting go of the hold I had on the belt, grabbing her hips tightly.

I pistoned into her, rutting like the beast I was, her pussy pulsating around my cock.

The only noises were our moans of pleasure and the flap of my skin against hers.

I closed my eyes and tilted my head up, grabbing her hips even tighter. I was sure I'd leave bruises, but I was too far gone to act rationally.

My cock got even harder as my balls drew close together. I was about to come but I wanted her to come at the same time, squeezing my cock.

I let go of one of her hips and circled her, starting to rub at her clit at the same rhythm as my thrusting and suddenly the walls of her pussy tightened almost painfully around my cock and she shouted my name. I closed my eyes, riding the tightness caused by her orgasm and followed her almost immediately.

I came for what seemed like forever, surprised that the force of my orgasm didn't just tear the condom.

I fell breathlessly against her back and kissed the back of her neck.

She tilted her head to the side, and I saw her small, satisfied smile. "It was the most earth-shattering orgasm I ever experienced," she said, her voice hoarse after all the screams of pleasure she'd let out as I pounded into her.

I grazed my teeth against the ball of her shoulder, not ready to leave the warmth of her body. "It was like nothing I ever experienced. You fed the beast now, Dolcetta; he'll want to keep on coming out to play."

She let out a happy sigh. "Then let him come out to play. I enjoy him."

I kissed the back of her neck again before reluctantly pulling out of her. I removed my condom and threw it in the bin behind me before reaching for her and lifting her gently from the table and carrying her to my room.

She nestled in my arms, closed her eyes, and

kissed my jugular before resting her head in the crook of my neck.

I was just too emotional to speak. She'd done it. She made me fall in love with her, and I was not sure I'd ever be able to let her go.

12

INDIA

I looked at Arabella as she grabbed my finger in her little hand, her eyes the same as Cassie and me.

"All clean, little girl..." I cooed at her after throwing away the stinky diaper. I turned toward Cassie who was feeding Marco in the rocking chair.

"That boy has one appetite." She chuckled, looking down at him with so much love in her eyes.

"They are growing so fast," I admitted, looking at the little girl in my arms. She smiled at me and tried to grab my plate. "Three weeks..."

"Yes, I still can't believe I've been a mom for that long already." She looked up and smiled. "I'm so grateful for your help."

"It's a pleasure, Cassie, really."

I put Arabella back in her bed and watched as she dozed off.

Soon enough I would not be needed here. Hell, I was barely needed now. I came to be with Cassie during her pregnancy. I hadn't expected to find everything that I've found, and now just the thought of leaving was too much.

"I don't get to do much now anyway. Luca is the perfect father. If it was not for him and Dom going to the city today, you wouldn't have needed me at all."

"Are you liking it here?" Cassie asked out of the blue.

I turned to her. "I do."

She chuckled, readjusting her breast and pressing her son to her shoulder to make him burp.

"Are you uncertain?"

"No, no, I do. I'm just not sure where this is leading."

She nodded. "It's obvious that you and Dom are close and that you are not..." She cocked her head to the side as if she was trying to figure out her next words. "You don't seem to mind the life we lead."

Cassie and I never really addressed me knowing the truth about Luca and Dom. I think part of her felt guilty for not sharing even if I knew it had not been her place to. Now we were just comfortable in our knowledge.

As for Dom and me, we were close—as close as he

allowed me to be at least. Since the night we'd shared in New York, I've shared his bed.

I was scared of it all, of all the feelings he woke up in me, but I was addicted. I couldn't tell him goodbye yet.

"Do I mind? I mean that's probably not the life I would have chosen, but Luca and Dom, they are good men, decent men with value, and that's all that matters to me."

She nodded with a small smile, as if I'd given the answer she expected.

"Why don't you stay?" she asked.

My heart leaped in my chest. I wanted nothing more than to stay. There was nothing good waiting for me back in Calgary.

"My plane is not for another two weeks."

"It's not what I mean. Why don't you stay... permanently?" she asked, standing up and putting Marco in his bed.

"I don't know. There are so many parameters to take into consideration."

"There is," Cassie agreed, grabbing the baby monitor and jerking her head toward the door. "But the most important part here is, would you want to?"

I followed her down the hall. "My willingness to stay here is not the only crucial factor. There's Luca, Dom, housing, and visas."

She waved her hand dismissively as we went down the stairs to the kitchen. "This house is humongous. You moving in will barely be noticeable, so that solves the housing." She turned toward me as we reached the kitchen. "Tea?"

I nodded mutedly.

She pointed at a stool. "Sit."

"Yes, ma'am!" I couldn't help but smile at her bossy attitude. She was the same with Luca and Dom, and seeing her tiny self order big bad Mafia men around was both funny and endearing.

"Luca really likes you and I told him I was intending to ask you to stay. He loved the idea." She turned the kettle on and turned around, setting a cup in front of me. "Luca wants nothing more than Dom's happiness and you're making him very, very happy."

I blushed at the compliment. I hoped I was making him happy, at least half as happy as he was making me, and knowing that both Cassie and Luca noticed that really made my day.

"He's making me happy too."

"I noticed and I love that for you." She grabbed a chocolate chip cookie she made the day before and bit a piece off. "So what do you say?"

I looked down at my cup, thoughtful. I wanted to stay; of course I did, but was it what Dom wanted?

"Is it your job? I thought you could do it just as well from here."

"No, I mean, yes, I can. It's a web-based therapy; I can do it from anywhere." I glanced at the clock. "I even have a new patient in twenty minutes. That's not the problem."

"Then what's the problem?"

"Dom."

"Dom?" She frowned, holding her cup halfway to her mouth. "I thought you liked Dom."

Like... I was way past *like* and that was the issue.

"Me liking Dom is not the problem. Dom and I, we're not discussing our relationship." I took a drink, trying not to show the extent of my embarrassment. "Who says Dom would like for me to stay?"

Cassie burst into laughter, and I looked at her with an eyebrow raised until she stopped laughing.

"I'm sorry!" She wiped at the tears under her eyes. "You can't be serious?"

I shrugged, taking a sip of my tea.

"Oh, India, no!" She put her cup down and rounded the counter to wrap her arms around me.

"Dom is crazy about you! We can see that. Luca and I can't stop talking behind your back about it."

I should have been annoyed at being the source of the couple's gossip, but I wanted to know what she saw; I needed her to give me hope that I was more than a temporary crush.

"Is he?"

"You can't see it? Really?"

I let out a sigh. I did, sometimes I really did, but then he never really made a commitment to me. "I don't know."

197

Cassie shook her head. "He took you around in New York right?"

"He did…" I trailed off, not sure where she was going with that.

"Okay, I know it's different from other men, but with the life they lead, they take relationships very seriously because as you can imagine, attachments can be seen as a weakness."

"Okay?" I was no expert of this whole Mafia life, but I could imagine that the more people you loved, the more open to retaliation you were.

"When Dom took you out, showing you around, he made a commitment to you."

I frowned. "It was just a couple of dates and a trip to a museum."

She shrugged, going back around the counter for her tea. "Maybe it is to you; maybe it is to a normal dating situation, but it's not like that in our lives. Everything is well thought out and considered. Dom would not have taken you out in public, showing a potential weakness to the world for no reason, especially knowing you are part of my family." She shook her head. "He made a commitment to you there, maybe not verbally, but I can assure you he did."

I nodded, taking a sip of the tea. "Okay, it's just all different, you know."

"It takes some time to adapt, I agree." She smiled. "I've been here for almost two years, and it's still weird sometimes." She cleared her throat. "Do you think you could adapt to this life?"

I couldn't help but smile a little at that; she was just as smooth as an elephant in a China store. "Are you fishing for information?"

She shrugged. "I'm just curious."

"I would appreciate it if this information stayed between us."

"I won't say anything to Dom," she added quickly, but I didn't miss she didn't mention Luca.

"I think that for the right person, I won't have any issue, no."

"Okay…"

I rolled my eyes. "Cassie, I'm serious, don—"

I was interrupted by a screaming infant coming full blast from the monitor.

"Ah, I'm sorry. It seems my daughter changed her mind about her feeding. Plus, you have to be ready for your new patient, right?"

I looked at the clock and nodded. I only had ten minutes left to connect and get ready.

Cassie sighed as we went up the stairs. "I swear that kid is already a diva; how is that even possible?"

I laughed. "Based on how her father is treating her? I'll be ready for years of princess attitude."

"She's so going to be a daddy's girl." She groaned but the comment lacked heat; she clearly didn't mind.

"Work on your son and make him a mommy's boy."

She winked at me. "Oh, don't you worry, that's my plan."

I watched her go to the second floor before going into my bedroom. I changed quickly from my nirvana t-shirt to a dress shirt, grabbed my glasses, and sat at my computer just in time for my new client to sign in.

Glen Franklin, 31, banker, suffering from social anxiety. Not the easiest for someone in that type of job.

I launched the session and froze when I met hazel eyes I used to find friendly but were nothing but hateful now.

"Did you really think you could escape me, India?" Jake cocked his head to the side, a sadistic smile on his face.

Cold sweat ran down my spine at his perfect face, his brown hair styled to perfection. He looked so nice, so acceptable in the eyes of society—the kind of man you wanted to date, the kind of man other women envied you for… If only they'd known the monster lurking beneath the surface.

I quickly looked up at the screen and the bleeping red light, the scene was recorded.

"India, I'm talking to you."

"Who's Glen?" The server was secured, identities were checked; he couldn't just…

He laughed. It was a laugh I used to like before I realized it lacked warmth, humanity. It was the laugh he used to give me when I was not doing what he wanted, the laugh that he gave me before striking.

"Glen is a loyal friend who is helping me track down my elusive girlfriend. Where are you, India?"

Girlfriend? The man was overly delusional. How could he ever think there'd be a turning back after the last time.

"I'm not your girlfriend," I replied, trying to remain cool and keep my voice from shaking. He didn't deserve my fear; he didn't deserve any type of feelings except my contempt.

He waved his hand dismissively on the screen. "That's something we need to discuss; you didn't even give me a chance to do so."

"What was there to discuss? You left me unconscious and bloody on the floor with a broken eye socket."

"Only because you didn't listen." He shook his head. "I *told* you, you couldn't go out with your friend. You chose to not listen. You know better now."

I shook my head. How did I ever put up with a man like him? How did I ever think it was what I deserved?

But now I knew better; now I had Dom, no matter for how long. I knew what it was like to be cherished and treated how I deserved. I could never go back to the hell I lived through with him.

"Come home, India. Don't make me come looking for you. You won't like it if you do."

I had to laugh at that. I could just imagine him walking into this Mafia compound... I didn't give him five minutes.

"Don't mock me, India!" he roared, slamming his hand on his desk. "I'll find you!"

"You can try," I shouted back, slamming my laptop shut and throwing it against the wall before I could think better of it.

I rested a trembling hand against my lips, letting out a tearless sob.

The door of my room opened briskly. Dom stood in the doorway, his eyes scanning the room, murder written all over his face.

"Dolcetta?" His deep voice made me feel safe in an instant. How was that possible?

I looked up and met his eyes, shaking my head mutely.

He crossed the room, pulled me up from my chair, and I was in his arms before I could take a breath.

He kissed the top of my head. "Talk to me, Dolcetta," he whispered against my ear, tightening his hold on me.

"Jake," I replied, burying my face in Dom's neck, taking in his woodsy cologne and faint cigar smell. The cigar was unusual, and I suspected he'd been with smokers. "He found a way to me," I added, closing my eyes and just letting Dom's unadulterated strength surround me.

He rubbed my back slowly, soothingly. "I know you're strong and your own woman and all that. And believe me, Dolcetta, I respect you like you have no idea, but you've got to let me do something." He kissed the side of my head, letting his lips linger on my temple. "I can't let my woman be upset like that and not intervene; you're asking too much of me here."

I froze and moved my head a little to look into his beautiful brown eyes full of concern.

"Your woman?" I asked tentatively. I really liked the sound of that.

He let out a long sentence in Italian that was just a series of insults before looking heavenward.

"Not really the way I wanted to discuss this."

"Discuss what?"

"Us. I came up to ask you to go away with me this weekend so we can talk about our relationship."

I looked at him with suspicion. "Have you talked to Cassie?" She was so dead.

He frowned. "No... Have you?"

"No?"

He let out a little chuckle. "These two I swear."

I let out a small laugh again and rested my head back against the crook of his neck.

"What do you say? Are we going away? I'd understand if you didn't want to, after that reminder."

"No, I do, actually even more now."

He let go of his hold of me and I felt the loss. I wanted to stay in his arms forever. He pulled me away a little and rested his hands on my shoulders.

"Good, it's settled. Now, what's his name?"

I bit my bottom lip. I was not sure that unleashing Dom on Jake was a good idea.

"I won't kill him."

I shook my head. "No, I know. Well, no, I don't know, but I didn't think you would. Not that it matters. Jake's not worth our time or the trouble."

"Dolcetta, it's not trouble; it's a duty and a pleasure. No one gets to upset you, do you understand?"

I smiled up at him and rested my hand on his cheek. "How is it you make me feel that special? That cherished?"

"Because it's what you deserve. Give me his name, Dolcetta. I could find out, but I want you to give me approval."

"No killing?"

"No killing," he confirmed with a sharp nod. "Maybe just a little mauling," he added with a cheeky grin.

"Jake Warner."

"Brava." He leaned in to peck my lips. "Be ready tomorrow at four. Pack light. I don't plan on us getting out of bed much."

"You're incorrigible," I chastised him, slapping at his chest playfully.

He grabbed my hand and kissed my palm. "No, *sono innamorato*," he said with a wink before exiting the room with a deep laugh.

Domenico Romano, killing machine, Mafia knight... but most of all, the man I was falling in love with.

13

DOM

I checked my travel bag one more time, making sure I took everything I needed for this weekend.

I had wanted to take India to the mountains—I really did—but with the crazy notes of my stalker and the rat we were no closer to find, I was completely stressed out.

But Luca convinced me to move on with India, that she deserved more than half-baked promises.

Of course she did. Fuck, the woman plain and simple saved me from the purgatory I'd been living in, and she didn't know it.

Luca was right. Being with me was her choice, but I needed to make my commitment clear, let her know that against all odds I'd found the one I never thought I'd find, and if she wanted to leave me, I would let her go, not showing the depth of the despair she would leave me in.

When we came back from New York, I went to her room to ask her to go away for the weekend when I heard her shout and my heart stopped. I wanted to kill whoever had been causing her that much distress.

Jake Warner... When she told me his name, giving me the approval to go after him, this man was as good as dead.

I had not lied to India; he was not going to die. Death was too sweet for a man like him, but he was going to suffer. He was going to be the prey for once and never again would he ever be the predator hurting women.

I had wanted to take care of him myself; it was personal. He'd hurt my girl. The fact that it happened before she was mine didn't matter. He'd touched something precious and he needed to pay.

All women were precious, and men like him were the scum of humanity.

But I had to put India first, our relationship, or rather what I wanted our relationship to become, and if I went to Calgary, I would never have been back for the weekend, so I called our Canadian famiglia and explained to him in great detail how I wanted him to take care of this abuser.

Come on, Jake Warner, try hitting women with two shattered hands and two replacement knees... I dare you.

I grabbed my bag and stopped by Luca's office. I rapped softly on the slightly ajar door and opened it to find Luca on his chair, looking lovingly at Arabella.

I looked at him for a second, so happy for my friend and what his life had become.

Luca looked up and quickly glanced at the clock on the wall.

"Aren't you supposed to be gone?" he whispered, rocking her in his arms softly.

"I'm on my way down. Isn't she a bit young to learn about the family business?"

"Cassie is taking a nap and Marco is sleeping. This little one didn't feel like sleeping and I didn't want her to wake up the whole house." He looked back down at his daughter and brushed his lips against her forehead. "Plus, it's never too early to learn. My girl is going to be the most majestic and feared Mafia princess in all of North America," he said reverently.

I believed him and I'd help him get her there.

"I just wanted to check if you needed anything before we left."

Luca rolled his eyes. "I can survive a weekend without you, Domenico. We discussed this before. When you can put her first, do it. These moments are rare, but when you have the chance, don't hesitate. You always had my back, brother; let me have yours."

I nodded, putting the bag on my shoulder.

"Get into the car, turn off your damn phone until Monday, and work on what makes you happy."

"Okay, I'll see you on Monday."

"*Si, In bocca al lupo!*"

I snorted but didn't reply, I sure needed all the luck I could get.

When I made it downstairs, India was already waiting for me by the door, her small black suitcase by her feet.

She was dressed in simple black skinny jeans with a red thermal shirt, her thick lustrous hair in a braid falling over her shoulder. She was absolutely stunning.

"Sorry, I didn't know you were already waiting." I leaned down to peck her lips, and once again I marveled at how easily I touched her and how she responded to me.

"I've been down only a couple of minutes. I wanted to see Cassie, but she is sleeping, and Lord knows she needs it."

I nodded, looking at her braid and already seeing myself wrapping it around my hand once we're in the cabin and— My dick twitched in my pants. Fuck, it was going to be a long drive up for sure.

She gave me a little smile, her green eyes darkening with both amusement and desire. Yep, she

knew what I was thinking and she was enjoying it...
My little minx.

"Let's go before I do something that will delay us greatly," I huffed, grabbing her suitcase and opening the door.

"You say that like it's a bad thing," she called after me.

"It's not." I opened the trunk and put our luggage in. "I just want to make sure we get to our destination first because I'm not sure that once I start, I'll be able to stop."

I didn't miss how she pressed her thighs together and how her nipples appeared under her thin shirt. This woman was going to be the death of me, and it was a death I'd welcome with a smile.

"Where are you taking me?" she asked curiously once we were settled in the car. "Not that it really matters," she added quickly.

I threw her a side-glance; she could not be serious. "How can it not matter? What if I took you to a dump in the middle of the woods?"

She shrugged. "We'll be together."

Fuck, here she was, slaying me again. I could feel my heart expand in my chest to the point of pain. There was no denying it; I was insanely in love with this woman.

I could not speak for a few minutes. The new inflow of emotions was still so difficult for me to process. I could fully understand Luca's addiction to

Cassie. This rush of feelings, this sense of belonging, this purpose... it was beyond addicting.

"Luca owns a cabin in the mountains about two hours up Ridge Point. We rarely use it because, as you can imagine, we can't go in the middle of nowhere often."

"No, but I'm glad we get to do it."

I reached over and grabbed her hand before bringing it to my lips for a quick kiss. "Me too, Dolcetta, me too."

We'd been driving for about an hour when my phone rang, and I cursed myself for not listening to Luca and turning it off.

I glanced at the screen. 'Genovese.' *In your dreams I'll pick up this call.* I pressed the reject button. He knew I was taking India away. Fuck.

"You know you can get it. I understand," she said gently. "I don't mind."

"You don't but I do." I shook my head. "This weekend is about you and me. Luca said for us to be successful, our relationship needs to be put first every once in a while, and this is one of those times." I turned off my phone for good measure. "Whatever it is, Luca can deal with it."

"Your *work* is important."

I didn't miss how she stumbled on the word. It was difficult for her to wrap her head around my way of living—how could it not—but she was willing to try, and that was all that mattered.

"You're much more important. You're saving me, India. Just like Cassie saved Luca."

She turned a little on her seat to look at me. "Cassie didn't save Luca, and I'm not saving you. Luca saved himself because of his love for Cassie. She was there by his side, loving him even when it was hard to, being his light when he needed it, but she didn't save him. He did." She let out a little laugh. "You're giving me a lot of credit and God knows I love you for it."

I threw her a little startled look. "Did you just say you loved me?

Her skin turned crimson as she widened her eyes at the realization of her words. "No..." she said, somehow dejected.

I shrugged. "Ah, that's too bad."

"Why?"

"Because I wanted to say that I loved you too."

"Oh." She looked out the window silently for a little while and I would have paid to know what was going through her head.

She started to laugh all of a sudden.

I frowned. "What?" Of all the things, I didn't expect our declaration of love to make her laugh.

"It's so us," she said in between giggles, wiping at her tears of laughter. "Nothing we do is normal... Same goes for our declaration of love."

I smiled at that. She did have a point. Our first sexual encounter had me attached to the bed. "You have a point… Let me make it better. *Te amo*, India McKenna."

"I love you too, Domenico Romano."

We made it to the small town before the cabin just as the sun started to set.

"We just need to pick up the food I ordered for us. Five minutes and we'll be on our way."

She frowned as we parked in front of a dimly lit convenience store. "It looks closed." She quickly looked around. "Actually, everything looks closed."

"It's a small town, and it's past six. Yes, everything is closed, but don't worry. I have contacts." I winked at her playfully. "I'll be right back."

She laughed. "I'll be waiting."

I hurried to the convenience store and knocked once. The older lady behind the counter came to open the door with a scowl on her face.

"You're late," she barked as soon as she unlocked the door.

"Sure am, ma'am. I'm sorry." That old bat had never been scared of our family and I respected her for that.

"Your food is here. It will be one hundred dollars for the food and fifty dollars for making me wait."

I laughed, reaching for the money in my wallet. Nothing could annoy me today. "You know what? Here is two hundred dollars, for the wait."

The old woman's face softened. "I appreciate it. Enjoy your weekend."

"I well intend to," I replied, making sure the whipping cream was in the bag. I was planning to use it on India tonight.

I exited the store with both bags in my hands and walked the few steps down the street just in time to see India get out of the car, her eyes wide.

"Dom!" she shouted just as I felt a sharp pain in my side.

I looked to my right side and saw a knife stabbed in my side. I looked up again, meeting blue eyes and a face I didn't know.

"For Emily," he growled before stabbing me again and again until everything went black.

14

INDIA

I decided to check my phone when Dom entered the store, and my heart stopped when I saw six missed calls from Luca. The man had never called me before.

I pressed call with shaky hands and he answered on the first ring.

"India, thank God. Where are you?" he let out on a huff.

"We're in a small town. Dom went to pick up some food for the weekend and—"

I heard a string of quick Italian coming from someone else.

Luca replied quickly to the other person before talking to me again. "India, listen. When he comes back, tell him to turn the car around. We're on our way."

"Luca, why? Oh, he's coming out now. Talk to him."

I opened my door to exit the car just as a blond man appeared by Dom's side.

Dom let out a cry as his shopping bags hit the ground, soon followed by his massive body.

"Dom!" I screamed, running toward him as the blond man turned around, a long bloody knife in his hand.

My phone fell on the ground, and I could hear Luca shout in the background.

"You should thank me," he said, looking down at Dom and the dark blood spreading alarmingly fast on the white sidewalk.

I reached in my bag for my taser and put it on his neck at full force, then I knelt on the ground as the man fell unconscious. "Luca, he's hurt!" I shouted, pressing one hand against Dom's wounds as I grabbed my phone and put it on speakerphone.

"We're about thirty minutes out, India. Do you see anything that could help?"

I looked around; the streets were dark and deserted—like in a bad horror movie. Like the horror movie my life was bound to be if Dom died on the pavement. My eyes stopped on a vet office with some dim light coming from the back.

"There's a vet. I'm not sure." I shook my head,

looking at Dom's paling face. He was dying there in the street, his blood soaking the white stones of the sidewalk slowly but still much too fast for me. I let out a tearless sob. "I'm going to lose him; Luca; please do something."

"You grab the gun in the holster of his left ankle, and you make that vet help. *Capiche?*" The voice I recognized now was the man from the hospital.

"I-I don't know how to use a gun." My mind was reeling; it couldn't be real—this couldn't be it.

"You don't have to; he just needs to think you can." The commanding coldness behind the man's words helped me keep my mind from being completely overwhelmed with worry.

He sounded so calm and composed; he had to know it would be alright.

"Okay, I can do this, but please come," I begged. I left the phone on the ground, grabbed the small gun on Dom's ankle, and ran to the glass door of the veterinary practice.

I banged my fist on the door, looking at Dom and the man on the ground.

Please, God, don't do it; don't take him away from me.

I let out a little cry of victory as a middle-aged man dressed in scrubs came to the door warily.

He opened the door slightly.

"Sorry, we're clo—"

I pushed the door with all my strength, making him stumble.

"He-he got stabbed! You have to help him now!" I asked, pointing a shaky, bloody finger toward Dom.

He looked and paled. "Ma'am, I'm not a doctor. I'm a veterinarian."

I pointed the gun at him, my hand shaking so much I was not sure I would have hit anything even if I wanted to.

"You have to help him now! There's no doctor."

The man raised his hands, looking from my shaking hand to my tear-stricken face.

"I'll try to help… Just put the gun down, miss. I'm not your enemy." He pointed at the back. "Just let me get the trolley cart we use for big dogs. I'll be right out."

I rushed back as the man on the floor started to stir. I tased him again for good measure and hoped the vet didn't lie to me and he was not in the back calling the police while the man I loved was bleeding out on the pavement.

"Don't leave me, Dom; we've got so much to discuss," I begged, pressing on his wound again.

My prayers were answered when the man appeared with the cart. "The nearest hospital is an hour away." He looked down at Dom. "He won't make it that long."

"I know," I replied, my voice breaking.

I helped the man put Dom on the cart.

"Is he the perpetrator?" he asked, jerking his head toward the blond man.

I nodded quickly.

"I have some binding in the back. Take care of him. I'll see what I can do for your friend."

"I have what we need." I let the man wheel Dom in the clinic while I rushed to the car to retrieve the pair of handcuffs I had in my back for the weekend... I expected to use them for something a lot more fun than trapping a murderer.

I put his arms behind his back and secured them with the handcuffs, then I grabbed him under his arms and pulled him into the clinic.

I was a tall, strong woman and it felt like the extra adrenaline from fear and anger was making me even stronger than I'd ever been.

"You can lock him in the quiet room. It's the door on your left," the man shouted at me.

I looked at him. He was leaning over Dom who was now lying on a metallic table in the middle of the room.

I locked at the man in the empty room, no bigger than a broom closet, before rushing in the room by Dom's side.

"How is he doing?" I asked breathlessly, standing close to the table. Nausea hit me as I noticed the four long wounds on Dom's side.

The man shook his head. "I'm not sure; I'm not a human doctor."

"He's all I have, please..." My voice cracked at the end as I rested my hand on Dom's cold cheek.

The man looked up at me, his eyes now only full of concern. He let out a sigh, jerking his head toward the side. "I need your help. Grab a pair of gloves and a mask and open the first drawers. There are long clamps that look like weird scissors; get three for me."

I nodded, acting mechanically, concentrating on my tasks and trying not to think of all that happened in less than ten minutes... How was that even possible?

I rushed back to the man and extended the clamps one by one.

"The man just attacked you?" he asked curiously as he widened one of Dom's wounds.

I looked away as my stomach churned viciously. This was most definitely different from *Grey's Anatomy*.

"Yes, I don't know him."

"Things like that don't happen in our small town, but you're lucky he was not very good. He missed his mark quite a few times. Hold this."

I turned toward him. "What?"

He nodded toward two of the clamps he was holding. "Only two of the wounds are dangerous. I need you to hold them tight to stop the blood flow."

"Okay." My hands were shaky as I approached the clamps.

"You need a steady hand; just calm down... He's going to be fine."

I knew he had no clue; he was just trying to humor me, but Dom's life could be depending on me.

I took a deep breath and forced myself to calm down.

I grabbed the clamps with a slight tremor.

The man started to move around, grabbing a machine and wrapping a band around Dom's wrist.

"Heart monitor, obviously not really fit for our purpose here, but that's the best I have." He turned toward the counter and grabbed a lot of things before placing them on a small tray which he wheeled back to us.

"I will start stitching inside where he nicked the artery. Just don't let go of the other clamp, okay?"

Did the man feel as defeated as he sounded?

"Will he wake up when you do that?"

"I gave him some sedatives. It's one for dogs but it works on humans; we should be okay."

"I can never thank you enough."

"Don't thank me yet; I'm not sure I can save him."

"Still, you're doing your best."

His eyes went down to the gun tucked in the waist of my jeans.

"I'd never hurt you. I don't even know how to use it," I admitted.

He simply took a deep breath and concentrated on the wound.

I turned my head as the bell of the door rang, and Luca and Matteo appeared in the room.

Luca's face was lined with worry, his eyes taking in the whole room, his face morphing in pure anguish at the shredded, blood-soaked piece of cloth on the floor that used to be Dom's shirt.

Matteo, the iceman, just stood tall, taking the room in with cool indifference. The look in his eyes, the coldness there, terrified me in ways Luca or Dom never could.

The vet looked up from his work and took a small step back.

"You are in no danger with us," Matteo's slightly accented voice sounded cold and harsh, so different from the pretend playfulness from the hospital. Somehow, I knew now that I was meeting the real man.

"As long as you do your best." He turned to me. "And as long as you remain faithful to us, we'll be on your side."

"Luca, we need help," I said to him, almost wishing he could take over and I could go cry in a corner for a bit. The adrenaline was wearing down and I felt like I would break down any minute.

"I know." He took a couple of steps toward us, keeping his eyes on Dom. "We've got people on the way, but it will take time."

The vet looked up. "He doesn't have time. He's lost too much blood. I'm not certain I can even close the second wound without blood."

"Then do a transfusion," Matteo piped up from his spot against the wall.

Luca sighed with exasperation, throwing him a glare.

The vet gestured to his room. "I'm a vet, not a surgeon. I have a transfusion machine but no human blood."

"Take mine," Luca offered, already taking off his jacket.

"No, I—" The man looked down at a white cart on the tray that had some blood on it. "He's AB negative." He jerked his head to the card. "The rarest blood type in the world. Less than one percent of the population has this type. Are you AB negative?" he asked Luca with hope.

Luca shook his head, looking at Dom again. "A positive," he replied, his face so dejected you would have thought he had been the one hurting Dom.

"Is he going to die without blood?" Matteo asked grimly, resting his eyes on Dom's form.

The vet winced. "I think so, yes."

Matteo cursed in Italian before removing his jacket. "Take mine," he commanded, rolling up his sleeve.

"Sir, if your blood is not perfectly compatible, this might kill him and—"

Matteo sighed in frustration, taking a few steps forward. "I'm AB negative too. I said, take mine."

I rested my hand on my chest, letting out a sigh of relief. I wouldn't have survived watching him die.

"Oh, thank God!" I looked at Dom, who was lying unconscious and scarily pale on the operating table. "What were the odds?"

Luca was silent, looking down with a frown as if he was trying to resolve a complicated math problem as the vet directed Matteo to a chair and started to hook him up to a weird machine that looked like a pump. The vet started to work on the machine. "I can't take more than three pints of blood or it will become dangerous."

"Would it be enough?" Matteo asked, looking down at his arm as the vet put the huge needle in it.

Matteo didn't even flinch as he stabbed his arm; seriously was this man a robot?

"I think temporarily yes, but he needs medical help, real help."

"It's on its way; just keep him alive."

It was not a request; it was very much an order, and the vet clearly got the message as he paled a couple shades.

He came back to my side, hooked Dom to the machine as well, and reached for the clamp.

"You did well. I'm taking over," he said gently, clearly having noticed I was just an exported piece on the chessboard. I was not a danger.

I nodded mutely, trying to unhook my cramped fingers from the clamp.

"You're in shock. Go behind the reception desk. There's Coke in the fridge. The sugar will help. And get the sandwich too and give it to your friend. He'll need it."

I looked at Matteo. *Friend...* somehow I felt like being friends with this man would be more a curse than a blessing.

I turned to leave the room when Luca suddenly looked up with wide eyes as if he'd just connected the dots on something.

"Brother, brother, where are you? I'm standing right next to you," he sang barely louder than a whisper.

I frowned, looking from one man to the other.

Matteo glared at him. "It's complicated."

"You..." Luca started.

Matteo shook his head. "Now is not the time." He pointed at the tube stuck in his arm, filling with blood. "Do you want to save your friend?"

Luca's glare turned murderous, his lips in a grim line. "Do you want to save your *brother*?"

I gasped. Brother? Dom was Matteo's brother? Did he know it?

"Half, actually," Matteo continued like it was not the revelation of the year.

"Does he know?" I asked, still in awe.

Matteo shook his head.

Luca crossed his arms on his chest, ready to take

over the world. "Did you know? When you *granted* me my favor?"

Matteo gave him a small smirk. "I never said your interests didn't meet mine."

Matteo turned to the small bottle half filled with his blood.

"If only I had that man."

"We do."

Both Luca and Matteo turned toward me.

"*Che?*" Matteo asked.

"I tased him." I pointed to the wall. "He's handcuffed and locked in the room there."

Luca and Matteo kept looking at me as if I just grew a second head.

Matteo turned to Luca. "*È meglio che la sposi. Perché non troverà qualcuno migliore.*"

I couldn't help but smile. "If he asks me, I'll say yes."

Luca looked at me with wide eyes. "You speak Italian?"

I nodded. I always loved learning languages, thinking I would one day travel the world with my mother.

"You never said!"

I shrugged. "You never asked."

Matteo let out a dark laugh. "*Lei mi piace.*"

He liked me? Again, I was not sure if it was a good thing.

"Nice try changing the subject, Genovese, but

we're not done talking about—" Luca looked positively murderous, but he was interrupted by the vet.

"I'm done," the vet huffed, removing his gloves and his mask before sitting heavily on his stool.

Luca turned to him. "Is he going to be okay?"

The vet ran a weary hand over his face. "I did the best I could with what I had. I think I stopped the hemorrhage, but he will need real medical attention soon."

"The ambulance with our team should be here any minute and we'll be out of your hair." Matteo's eyes turned colder. "And it's because I appreciate what you did that I'm granting you the benefit of the doubt and I'm letting you walk away."

I looked at him, mouth agape. Was he actually threatening an innocent man who just saved Dom's life?

I was ready to tell him to get fucked when Luca spoke.

"Matteo..." He turned toward the vet who was pale as a ghost. "Nothing will come to you. You'll be rewarded handsomely for your help."

The vet shook his head. "I don't want your money. The only reward I want is for you all to go and never come back." He turned toward Matteo. "I won't say anything to anyone, as far as what happened here tonight. An animal was injured and I patched him up."

Matteo nodded approvingly. "Perfect. As long as

this remains your story, we would not have a problem, and it's not that far from the truth actually."

"Hey!" I couldn't help but call out.

He sent me a side-look. "Defensive? Good to
know."

I crossed my arms on my chest and looked away.
At least part of me was grateful for him; while I was
being annoyed at him, I was not worrying
about Dom.

The vet removed the machine from Matteo's arm.
He stood up, swaying a little.

Luca took an instinctive step toward him.

Matteo raised his hand. "No, Gianluca. I'm fine. I
don't need help."

I didn't need to be a psychologist to know that
this man was cocky and full of himself to the point of
impertinence. He would never ask for help even if it
cost him greatly.

He grabbed the sandwich I left for him and bit
into it, grimacing as he chewed. "It's just plain ham?
Not even pastrami?" he asked the vet. "What are you?
A monster?"

I couldn't help but let out a little bark of laughter.
This seemed like being in another dimension, the
cruel Mafia boss drawing the line at a ham sandwich?

At that moment, three men came in with a
stretcher.

"Ah, the team is here."

"Would you like to go with him in the ambulance?" Luca asked me as the men started to work on getting Dom on the stretcher.

"Is it okay?" I was grateful beyond words. "But... what about his car?"

Luca gave me a small smile before reaching for my arm and rubbing it gently. "I'll drive it home. You go and be with Dom. You're the one he'll want by his side."

"Yeah?" I looked at the team wheeling Dom outside. "How can you be sure?"

"Because if it was me, I'd want no one other than my Cassie."

My heart swelled with love. Did Dom really see me like Luca saw Cassie? One could only hope.

"Yes, and I've a passenger I need to take back to the compound and have a chat with," Matteo added darkly.

And I knew it probably meant that man was never going to be seen alive again, and as chilling as it was, I was okay with that.

If I had to lose a little of my humanity to join his world, it was a sacrifice I was willing to make. He was worth it.

15

DOM

I tried to turn on my side and winced. I clearly couldn't be dead; it was too painful.

"Dom?"

I sighed when I felt a cool hand on my forehead.

"Dolcetta?" I barely recognized my own voice on how gravely it sounded.

"What happened?"

"Do you remember getting stabbed?"

Yes, that I remembered... I also remembered him calling a name I had done everything to forget.

I looked around the room and frowned. I was in my bed. How?

"How long ago?"

She sighed, sitting on a chair across from my bed. I finally noticed how tired she looked, with dark circles under her beautiful eyes, the taut lines of worry etched on her face.

"Two days, but they've been long."

"Tell me what happened."

And she told me the story. I felt horrible for putting her through all of that, risking her life to restrain the man and then committing a felony by threatening that vet to save me.

She could have gone to jail or worse, been killed by that man.

I loved her; that much was clear, but my life was tainting hers.

"I'm sorry."

She leaned forward on her chair, a frown between her eyebrows. "Why?"

Couldn't she see it? "For putting you through all this."

She shook her head. "None of it matters. You're here, alive. It was all worth it."

I sighed, looking toward the door. I was not worth it, and the man had every right to kill me for what I did to that poor girl so many years ago... He didn't deserve to be punished, I did.

"Dom, please, don't retreat into your mind. Talk to me. Don't shut me down."

"Is Luca here?"

She looked down at her hands, clearly a little deflated.

"Yes, Matteo is here too."

"Is he? Why?"

She shook her head and stood up, her face suddenly closed up and wary.

"I'll tell them you're awake. I'll bring you some food and drink."

I didn't want her to leave angry. I twisted in my bed and groaned at the pull on my side.

The wary look on her face turned to concern. "I'll get you painkillers too," she added quickly before slipping out of the room.

Fuck, why did I always have to blow it?

Because you're a self-destructive asshole.

I winced as I sat down, looking at the bathroom door just a few feet from me like it was ten miles out.

I got up, putting pressure on the bandage on my side, and walked slowly to the bathroom. I used the toilet, washed my hands and face, and was half tempted to give myself a shave. I really disliked looking unkempt, but my hand was shaking a bit too much to risk it.

Ask her, she'd be happy to do it. I shook my head trying to smother that little voice so eager to get its redemption.

When I walked back into my room, Luca and Matteo were already there. Luca was sitting on the chair India occupied before, and Matteo was leaning against the door, looking as bored as he usually was.

"Please make yourself at home," I said sarcastically.

"Well, it is so…" Luca shrugged before pointing at the nightstand. "India got that ready for you."

I looked at the platter and smiled. These were all my favorites.

"She's a good one," Luca commented with a small nod. "She saved your life."

I winced when I sat on the bed, the stitches hurting like a bitch.

"Painful?" Matteo asked, looking up from examining his nails.

I pursed my lips and gave him a sharp nod. I didn't want the fucker to know how badly it actually hurt.

He gave me a mocking smile. "Good, it'll teach you to not pick up your fucking phone." He glared at me. "Since when are you ignoring my calls? Did the boy grow a pair?"

I snorted. "I always had a pair and I was busy."

He arched an eyebrow. "Yes? Planning to fuck your girl? How did that work out for you?"

I let out a growl. I hated how dismissive he sounded. It was much more than just a simple fuck.

"India said you were on your way to the cabin. How did you find out?"

Luca gestured to Matteo.

"Well, if you'd taken one minute to answer your phone, you'd have known that the feeler I'd put out came through and the key of the safe was one of a small pawn store on 43rd Street." He reached in his pocket and retrieved his cell. He turned it toward me to show a small consignment box open. "There wasn't much in it. A copy of the *Art of War*, a burner phone with some texts, and a file with photos of a man and details about some of your activities when you were younger."

My heart squeezed painfully in my chest at the reminder—a reminder I didn't really need to be honest; I was living daily with this guilt.

"It's helpful though," Matteo continued, oblivious to my turmoil or maybe he just didn't care which was actually the most likely option. "Not a lot of people in the famiglia know about your father's hobbies or what he subjected you to. Once it became too messy, we ensured that most, if not all the lower men who knew anything were gone."

"Which means that the rat can only be a high member of the famiglia."

I scratched at the tattoo on my chest, the symbol of a loyalty that was being broken at the highest level. "That's not ideal."

"No," Matteo admitted, "but it's useful. These people are fewer."

That was true, and I knew Matteo was a man on a mission. He'd never stop until that rat was dead.

"The man who stabbed me. Did he say something?"

"Nothing useful."

"Who is he for her?" I asked almost reluctantly.

"Was," Matteo replied darkly. "Her brother."

I shook my head. "You shouldn't have killed him; he had the right to take his revenge. She killed herself because of what I did to her. I deserved it. He had every right to avenge his family."

"Just as I have the right to protect mine," Matteo replied sharply.

"We're part of the Mafia, Matteo. We're not family, not that way."

Luca leaned back on his chair, resting his right ankle on his thigh. "Matteo, talking about family..." He trailed off.

Matteo gave him a wicked smile, and I knew it was going to sting. "Yes, family... Tell him the truth, Gianluca. Tell him why you stepped up at fourteen. Tell him why you sacrificed yourself."

Luca glared at him. "That's not the point, Genovese. This is not what I'm talking about."

I turned to Luca. He was a lot of things but not an avoider. "You never said actually. In all these years, you never said what changed your mind."

Luca looked away, as if my chest of drawers was fascinating.

"Tell me, Luca," I insisted. I was not backing down this time. "You always said you wanted to wait until the last moment before joining the famiglia officially. That you were not ready to live by their rules and then you turn fourteen and just join them. Why?"

"Tell him, Gianluca," Matteo taunted. "Tell him how you begged me to let you kill him."

My heart stopped as my blood ran cold. Of all the people. "You took out my father?"

Luca gave me a sad look. "I had no choice, after I found out what he did to you. What else could I do?"

"How?" I asked, still disbelieving. It was not possible, why would the council… Why would Genovese allow that?

Matteo laughed. "He gave up his freedom."

I looked at Luca with confusion as dread settled in the pit of my stomach.

"What did you do, Luca?"

"He gave me a favor in exchange for convincing the members of the council to go his way and authorize his induction kill as your father."

My mind was reeling. Luca stepped up to the role he didn't want for me? The simple son of a made man?

I opened my mouth but no sound came out. I was too shocked.

"The favor you may ask?" Matteo continued, enjoying the potential pain he was causing us, the sadistic bastard. "To take any woman that was promised to me for himself."

I grimaced. "Francesca?"

Luca looked grim as he gave me a sharp nod.

"Oh, but that's not all, is it, Gianluca?" Matteo's smile was now downright predatory. "What did you have to do to convince your father?"

Luca glared at him. "We're done."

"No, I don't think so. He stepped up for you. Bowed down to his father, promising to follow his lead."

"You gave all that up for me?" I hardly believed it was possible.

Luca looked at me like I was an idiot. "You're my best friend. Of course I did, and there was not a day I regretted it. I had to save you."

"Ahhh, I would cry if I had feelings," Matteo mocked.

It was Luca's turn to smile at Matteo. "Now it's your time, isn't it? Do you want to do it or should I?"

Matteo shrugged like he didn't care, but I'd seen him come undone before. I recognized the signs, in particular the tick of his jaw. Now that I knew the signs, he couldn't hide anymore.

"So I found out that Matteo here had an ulterior motive to let me help you. Apparently, he had a hard time saying no to save his brother."

"Half brother," Matteo corrected.

"Who's half—"

I stopped dead, turning sharply toward Matteo. Him? I shook my head; it had to be a joke. I looked back at Luca who gave me a sharp nod. The look in his eyes was enough to tell me that it was anything but a joke.

"My father was your father too?"

Matteo curled his lips in disgust. "Fuck no! Like I would ever want to share genes with that low-life, messed-up scum."

I was still too surprised to mention how ironic of him to call anyone 'messed-up.'

"No, your mother was a friendly woman... who liked to spread love."

It was a nice way to say my mother was a prostitute.

"My father met her during a trip from Italy and well..." Matteo smirked. "Geneovese's charms are hard to resist."

"Charms? Is that what you call coercion and blackmail?" Luca asked, easing some of the tension.

I threw Luca an amused look as Matteo gave him his middle finger.

"The man who raised you didn't appreciate that his girl cheated on him." He shook his head. "I think he married her and claimed the child as a punishment to her and to him."

"How?" I shook my head. "When did you find out?" I hated him even more for letting me suffer.

"When Gianluca requested the right to kill your father, this is when my father told me."

"And you didn't think it was worth sharing?" I asked sarcastically.

"No, I did not." He sighed, rolling his eyes. "I saved your life. I gave you blood. Can we just move on?"

"You—" I turned to Luca. "He saved me?"

Luca opened his mouth to answer, but Matteo interrupted him.

"Why are you so surprised?" Matteo's voice was laced with irritation.

I turned toward him. "Because you're a psycho only caring about your own interests."

"Inaccurate and also you're my blood... you're my interest."

"This is—" I leaned back on my bed. "I need some time, alone."

"Fine, but once you're better, we'll need to discuss why you hid all the threatening messages you got," Matteo started, his hands on the handle. "And before you insult me, or him by saying you have no idea what we're talking about, we saw the texts in the flip phone that was in the consignment box."

I turned to Luca who looked more disappointed and hurt than angry which somehow hurt me a lot more.

"Luca..." I started, not sure how to make it better with my best friend. "I just— You were worried about Cassie and the babies and—"

"You're my family too, Domenico; losing you would hurt me."

"Oh, my heart..." Matteo wiped fake tears from under his eyes. "This is so beautiful."

"Vaffanculo!" I barked.

Matteo arched his eyebrows. "Remember your place, Domenico. I'm not just anyone."

"No," I agreed. "But the same Genovese blood that runs in your veins, runs in mine too… Remember that." I smirk. Because the secret brother of our king was bound to be fun.

"Being related won't save you." He was suddenly so serious. "Betray me and you'll die."

That sobered me up. "I'll never betray the famiglia."

"I know that; you're infuriatingly loyal."

"Why is loyalty infuriating? I thought you craved it."

"I am, but your loyalty is not to me." He looked at Luca. "And I can't figure out why."

I looked at him with my eyebrows arched. Had he just missed the part about Luca selling his freedom to save me?

I sighed and winced again as the pain in my side really started to act up.

Luca looked at my untouched tray of food and the bottle of painkillers. "Eat and rest, Dom. We'll talk about all that later."

I nodded gratefully; it was too many secrets revealed all at once. I really needed time to process it all.

I was not the son of the monster. Well, at least not that type of monster, not the worst kind of them and that changed so many things. I didn't have this twisted evilness running in my veins. Maybe I did have a chance at redemption. Maybe I could be happy, and I was smart and humble enough to know India was that chance.

I just had to be brave enough to show her all the sides of me and let her walk in with her eyes open.

Please, India, be the strength I need to save myself.

16

DOM

Three days. That's how long I waited for India to come back and see me. Matteo left the day I woke up with a promise or a threat to get me to the city for more rat sniffing.

Cassie came with the babies a couple of times, but I couldn't get India out of my mind and how dismissive I'd been of her.

Was she mad at me? Did she finally realize the sacrifices it meant to be with me?

The evening of the third night I decided it was enough. The pain in my side was much better even if the stitches still pulled like a bitch every time I moved. Going to the bathroom was a challenge but it was far from being the worst pain I ever experienced, and right now the pain of not seeing India or knowing where she stood with us was much more painful and unsettling. I loved that woman and if she was done with us, I had to know.

When I was done waiting for her, I got out of bed and dragged my shirtless ass out of the room and down the corridor to her room and I opened her door without knocking... Mad for mad.

She was sitting up in her bed, a book in her hands. When she saw me, she rested her book on her bed and smiled up at me.

"Dom, you're up!"

The weight of apprehension eased a little bit on my chest; she seemed happy to see me.

"I've missed you," I admitted, I was man enough to tell her that.

"I did too but I realized you needed your space." She rested her hands on her lap, looking at me with her soulful eyes.

"I don't need space, not from you, never from you."

She patted the empty space beside her and my chest eased completely. I couldn't help but marvel that after all of this, she still wanted me.

"How are you?" she asked after I settled beside her, my back against the headboard.

I followed her eyes to the bandage on my side. "Physically or mentally?"

She let out a little laugh. "Both, either, whatever you are ready to share."

I grabbed her hand, intertwined our fingers together, and kissed the back of it. "I don't deserve you."

"I'll be the judge of that, and I think you do."

I sighed, resting my head on the headboard, looking at the ceiling.

"I love you," I admitted, squeezing her hand tighter. "What happened didn't change that; it made me love you even more if at all possible."

"Okay?" She sounded so confused and how could she not be? I was confused as hell myself.

"But I can't help but think that it's going to be too much for you, that this life... You don't deserve this life."

"Don't you think I should be the judge of that?"

I turned my head toward her. She was studying me, her mouth pursed. I had annoyed her; that much was clear.

"You should, of course you should. I would never take that choice away from you, and that's what I wanted to talk to you about at the cabin."

She leaned against me, resting her head on my shoulder. "I'm here now; I'm listening."

I leaned my cheek against the top of her head as

apprehension on what I was about to do filled me. My past just resurfaced, and nothing guaranteed it would not come up again, and even if I hate that part of me, she had to get in this relationship with both eyes open.

"Maybe it's a good thing I didn't get to speak with you that day because I wanted you to stay for the man I am now, and I realized that you can't until you know the man I've been."

She remained silent and I was somehow grateful that she did.

"I have no right to complain; I never had the right. I'm not trying to justify what I did or excuse what I did, what he made me do when I was thirteen. What he made me do that day, it didn't kill me, but part of me died that day and has been chipping away ever since."

She squeezed my hand tightly, and it was my lifeline at this moment as I was about to dive in and share my darkest memories.

"The man who raised me, Sergio Romano, was not a good man. My mother was a call girl who he wanted and forced to marry." I closed my eyes at the pain the memories caused. I was grateful India could not see my face right now. "He didn't treat her well." Understatement of the year. "And she ended up ending her life when I was still very young." I instinctively wrapped my arm around India, pulling her closer to my body. Her presence alone made me feel better. "There are many rules in the Mafia, you see. Some are mandatory; others are more subtle, sort of guidelines... But my fa—" I stopped; he wasn't my father.

"It's okay to still see him as such. You believed he was your father for over thirty years." She kissed my neck before settling quietly again with her head in the crook of my shoulder.

"He started to kidnap some women and sell them. Others—the younger ones—he was drugging them, making them addicts and placing them into underground sex clubs." I couldn't help the bile that rose up my throat. "Men always paid more for underage women. But virgins are a little too messy. Men are not keen on the blood so my father was enjoying breaking them and making me watch. It was what real men had to do, you know? Take what they wanted no matter what the woman wanted." I took a deep breath as I was getting to the most horrible part of my history. "And then I turned thirteen and my father decided it was time for me to help in his mission. Her name was Emily; she was fifteen years old at the time, and my father gave me the choice—either I did it or he'd make his most monstrous man do it instead." I stopped talking for a few seconds, trying to rein in the turmoil inside me.

She let go of my hand and wrapped her arm across my chest. I'd expected her to shy away from me in disgust once she realized the monstrous things I'd done.

I looked down at her arm around my body, her flawless skin that felt like silk across my calloused fingers. I trailed my fingers up her arm slowly, enjoying the feel of her skin. Touching her was something I knew I'd never get tired of.

"The man who stabbed me—he had every right to do it. He was Emily's brother. Emily, she was never the same after that day. She got more and more into drugs until she killed herself the day she turned eighteen... eighteen." I shook my head and let out a defeated sigh. "I've watched my father hurt countless women, and I've hurt six girls... six until Luca did the thing I'd been too chicken to do and took him out." I swallowed through the lump in my throat. "I'm a rapist, India. Nothing I will ever do and nothing I'll say will ever change what I did or what I became. I've tried to atone for my sins for years and until you, I never thought I could get peace, but then I looked into your soulful eyes and the guilt, the pain faded... and you became right then the most important person of my life."

She took a sharp intake of breath, and I could feel her rapid heartbeat against my side. The problem was by not seeing her face, I didn't know if it was fear or otherwise.

"I hoped that finding out that Sergio was not my father would somehow help, that I was not wired to be a monster, that I didn't share DNA with the scum of the world, but it didn't, not really." I took a deep breath and kissed the top of her head, inhaling the faint jasmine scent of her shampoo. "I am a monster, India, because despite everything I want you to stay here, with me, forever. Despite my past, my sins, despite the life I lead which is full of danger, blood and death, I want you to stay and love me. I want you to stay so my love for you can save the remainder of my soul." I looked up at the ceiling, trying to stop myself from breaking down and shamelessly begging her to sacrifice herself to be with me despite not being worthy. "If I were a better man, I'd send you away to live a peaceful quiet life back in Calgary. I would wish for you to find a lovely husband, have kids, thrive, and be the amazing woman you are in the open, always safe. But I'm not a good man, and I love you... I'm addicted to you... I burn for you."

She moved into my arms, and I tightened my hold on her. I was not ready for her to pull away or look at me. I was not ready to see whatever her eyes conveyed.

"I don't want you to answer now. I want you to think long and hard about what a life by my side means. It's not an easy life; there will be times when you hate it... maybe even hate me a little, but I can promise you that I will revere you, protect you with everything I am, and love you until my last breath and even beyond that if I have my say in this. Stay with me, India."

I waited a couple of seconds, my heart pounding in my chest as I loosened my hold on her.

She got out of my arms and moved to look at me, her face strangely peaceful but not giving much away.

"It's late."

My heart sank in my chest; she wanted me to leave her to her thoughts. I nodded, moving from my spot on the bed. "Yes, of course, I—"

"Just get under the covers and hold me, Dom," she said with a small smile before turning to her side and putting her glasses on the night table.

I stayed up, looking at her back with incredulity. She wanted me to sleep with her? After everything?

She reached behind her and moved the cover.

I joined her slowly, still disbelieving. I slid close to her, wrapping my arm around her waist and pulling her close to me, her back flush against my chest where she belonged.

She turned off the light and let out a sigh of contentment as she relaxed in my arms, nestling even closer to me.

"Are you not even going to say anything?" I asked in the darkness.

She moved her hand to rest it on my arm around her. "Whatever I will say you won't listen. You're too caught up in yourself to see it… to see yourself as I'm seeing you, as everybody is seeing you. But we'll talk. We will but for now I just want to sleep in your arms where I feel safe. I need my eight hours of beauty sleep, Domenico. Not everyone is looking hot like you are naturally."

I smiled and kissed the top of her head. "Whatever you want, Dolcetta, whatever you want," I whispered before falling asleep, lulled by the gentle movement of her peaceful breathing.

———

When I woke up India was already gone, and once again I was taken aback by how deeply and peacefully I slept when she was by my side.

My life, my job, and my mind kept me on high alert, waking up at every noise, but not when I was with her. When she was secure in my arms, I was at peace.

I felt so much better today. I guessed all I needed was a good night with the woman I loved by my side.

I went back to my bedroom, took a shower, and finally was able to shave and trim my goatee— looking like myself again.

As I walked downstairs, I noticed how quiet the house was.

I made myself an espresso and was just sitting at the table when Luca appeared from the back door, dressed down in a pair of blue jeans and a white t-shirt.

"Morning, sleeping beauty." He grinned at me. "I was just about to come to wake milady."

I flipped him the bird as I sipped the caffeinated goodness.

"Where are the girls?"

"Sitting in the garden, they want to have a barbecue for the four of us."

I looked out the window at the bright sun and faint breeze in the trees. It seemed like a good day for that.

"You look well," he said with clear relief, leaning against the counter.

"I am, this woman…" I was at a loss of words; how could I say what India meant to me?

"I know." He looked toward the back door. "I feel the same for Cassie."

I sighed, leaning back on my chair. "The other day I didn't get a chance to really ask questions."

"Yeah, I expected that much." He pointed to the coffee machine. "Let me grab a coffee and let's take it to the library. Do you want another one?"

I stood up. "Sure."

I followed Luca to the library and sat on the green velvet chair across from him.

"Is he still alive?" I asked, already knowing the answer.

Luca looked away before shaking his head.

"Matteo is not forgiving when people touch who he considers to be part of his circle."

I grimaced. Matteo Genovese was my brother, how could I even deal with that.

"Did the man say something?"

Luca crossed his legs and shrugged. "I was not there when Matteo *interrogated* him. It's something he really enjoyed, and I was much more worried about you."

"If anyone can get the truth out of anyone, it's Matteo," I said, hating to admit it.

Luca took a sip of his coffee. "The man didn't know much. He received a file with all the details in regard to his sister and you. He left the notes on your car, but he was not the one texting you." He rubbed his fingers across his lips. "Talking about the messages. This is not something I should have found out from Matteo, Dom."

I looked down in shame, not able to stand the hurt etched in his eyes. "I wanted to tell you, I did, but Luca, you've already done so much for me. I wasn't sure it was something worht bothering you with."

"Dom, *i tuoi problemi sono i miei problemi.*"

Your problems are my problems. I took a deep breath and looked up. "You sacrificed the little childhood you had left for me, Luca. How—"

"And you stayed with me for two years, taking abuse and insults day after day just to make sure I didn't kill myself. We're family; that's what family does. We took an oath, remember?"

I nodded sheepishly. I knew that hiding the truth from Luca had been a mistake—of course I did—but things had been going so well for him.

"Just promise that no matter what, you won't hide anything else. Whatever it is, we will deal better if we do it together."

"I promise." I took a sip of my coffee and looked down at my cup. "So nothing really came out of it, did it?"

Luca gave me a half smile. "Not necessarily." He reached for his phone in his pocket, scrolled for a few seconds, and turned it to me. "Matteo sent me that yesterday."

I looked at the list of twelve names that I knew— they were all men of the famiglia. "Okay?"

"They are the only ones who knew enough about your father's side business to tell."

I glowered down at the list; one of them was our traitor, and once I found him…

"Does Matteo have a plan?"

Luca chucked. "When does he not? The guy is the master calculator. I suspect every action and every word coming out of his mouth is done with ulterior motives."

"And that man is my brother… yay."

Luca cocked his head to the side, signaling he was deep in thought. "I hate to admit it, but he stepped up as soon as he realized you needed his help, and he was frantic when he made it to the house, well as frantic as a man like him can be. I never thought I'd ever say it, but I think that Matteo Genovese really cares about you."

I snorted. "The man cares for no one but himself. He always says *'loyalty runs deeper than blood.'*"

"He does say that," Luca agreed. "I'm just not so sure he means it."

I shrugged. It was irrelevant now anyway. There were so many things I had to deal with before this, and one of them was India.

"I need to talk to you about India," I started. I had asked her to stay before checking with Luca. It was his home, and I didn't even take into account the dynamics.

"India is also something that came out from all of this. She is impressive, you know. She stepped up and defended you fiercely. She even stopped the man who stabbed you."

My heart stopped. India put herself at risk? For me? I let out a low growl. That's something we would have to discuss. No more putting herself at risk... for anything. She was much too precious for this.

"She impressed Matteo; he approves of her."

Not that it really mattered. I would fight the famiglia to keep her, but knowing that our king approved of her made things a whole lot easier.

"I asked her to stay here, with me. Permanently."

"Goddammit!" Luca blurted out.

"Listen, Luca, if this is a problem, we can move out. I—"

He waved his hand dismissively. "That's not the issue, *idiota*. Of course she can stay here forever; she's family. I just lost one hundred dollars to Matteo of all people, and that pisses me off."

I looked at him with an eyebrow raised. "Care to explain?"

He rolled his eyes. "After the incident, Matteo bet you'd ask her to stay before the week is out. I expected you to be a little slower and conflicted and to ask her on her way back to the airport. He won and I hate that."

"Betting on my life?"

Luca crossed his arms on his chest. "Annoying, isn't it?"

I pursed my lips. I'd done it to him too when he was toeing his way around Cassie. "That's fair."

Luca leaned forward and patted my shoulder with a laugh. "I'm happy for you, brother; she's a good woman. She'll make you happy."

"I'm just waiting for her answer."

He frowned. "She said she had to think about it?"

"No, I asked her to think about it. This is a serious decision she'll be making, with lots of responsibilities."

"Yeah, I did the same with Cassie, but the woman

is so deeply in love with you. I can't see her saying no."

I let out a humorless laugh. "For my sanity? I hope you're right."

Because I was wise and smart enough to know that India McKenna was my chance at happiness, my shot at redemption.

17

INDIA

I looked at the clock once more, smoothing my hand on the see-through red lace nighty I was wearing.

Luca had texted me an hour ago saying that Dom was on his way and my nerves have been growing exponentially since then.

I had wanted to make my answer to him a great gesture, to show him that I loved him and what he meant to me.

Men were always expected to be the ones doing all the romantic stuff, making a big declaration of love, getting down on his knee to propose, and I agreed—most times—but no, Dom deserved the grand show. He needed to see that he was deserving of all the love in the world and that it was not only his role to make me feel cherished, but it was my role too. As his woman I needed to show him that he also was a treasure even if he doubted so himself.

I made him wait the whole week for my answer, and I knew that the more I waited, the more anxious he got, but I wanted the moment to be special to make a commitment to him.

Luca sent him to see Matteo in the city but asked him to stop at the condo first where I was waiting, wearing nothing more than the short lace nighty and a G-string.

My heart stalled as I heard the beep announcing the arrival of the private elevator.

I took a deep breath, arranged my hair in loose curls around my face, and leaned against the stool as sexily as I could, trying to hide my nerves.

Dom walked in, his head down, muttering in Italian. He stopped in his tracks when his eyes connected with the rose petals on the floor.

He looked up and let his bag fall in a loud *thump* as his eyes widened and his mouth hung open in shock.

I smiled at him, regaining confidence from his reaction. I mentally patted my own back. I'd picked well.

"Did I die and go to heaven?" His hooded eyes trailed up my body, stopping at the small piece of fabric covering my pussy, and then stopping at my breast, my nipple puckering under the heat of his gaze. He licked his lips as his eyes stayed on my chest, and I could almost feel his warm tongue on my breast.

He took a couple of steps toward me. "My God, India, Dolcetta, you're slaying me." He let out a painful growl. "Please tell me I don't have to go see Matteo now because there's no way I'll be able to walk out of this apartment."

I shook my head, the emotion much more overwhelming than I expected. We didn't have sex since he got stabbed and I wanted him right now just as much as he wanted me.

"Thank fuck," he whispered before falling to his knees in front of me. He grabbed my right ankle gently and brought it up and kissed the inside of it.

I gasped, grabbing the stool behind me as his lips burned my skin.

He brushed his nose gently up my leg, kissing it along the way until my knee was resting on his shoulder. He stopped when he reached my quivering inner thigh and bit me gently.

I let out a moan, spreading my legs a little more.

He let out a little tsk when his nose brushed the silk of my G-string. "That won't do, Dolcetta. You can't hide my favorite dessert," he whispered against the silk, his hot breath and his words making me even wetter.

He hooked his forefinger under the fabric and pulled it to the side, baring me to him.

I gripped his coarse hair as he tasted me with his long, flat tongue.

He let out an animalistic growl as his free hand came up and grabbed my ass in a bruising hold. I enjoyed it, the mix of pain from his hand and the pleasure of his tongue.

He pulled me closer to his face, burying his mouth in my soaked folds, pushing his tongue into my tight channel.

He licked the length of my slit again. "You taste so good." He moaned against my clit, sending vibrations all over my body.

I looked down at him and met his hungry eyes. Seeing this big, powerful, and scary man kneeling in front of me, pleasuring me with his tongue made it even more intoxicating.

And suddenly as he nipped at my clit, I came, screaming his name.

He rested his hands on my hips as he came up, his hair tousled by my fingers, his lips glistering with my juice.

He kept his eyes on mine as he licked his lips greedily and that alone almost made me come again.

He cupped my tender pussy possessively. "I need to be inside you now."

"Yes, please. Take me; I'm yours... always."

His eyes widened ever so slightly, probably

understanding the meaning of my words, but he was just as overcome by desire as I was.

He leaned over and pulled me into his arms, carrying me bridal style to the bedroom.

He put me on the bed and took off his jacket, shirt, pants, and underwear, keeping his eyes on me, studying my every move.

I let my eyes trail down to his erect cock bobbing close to his belly button. This man was a work of art in every way.

He crawled on the bed and hooked his fingers on the side of my G-string, pulling it down.

He hooked it on his finger and looked at it. "I like it, but I prefer your pussy bare."

I opened my legs wider and was satisfied at the low guttural sound of approval coming from deep in his chest.

He threw my underwear on the floor and crawled over me, pulling my nightgown along the way.

He leaned down and took one of my nipples in his mouth, suckling at it.

I hissed, arching my back.

"Mine," he muttered as he let go of my nipple.

"Yours," I agreed as he concentrated on my other nipple.

"Forever," he added as he let his lips trail up my neck.

"Forever, yes." I raised my hips, seeking the friction of his heavy cock against my clit. "I want you, Dom."

He grabbed the base of his cock, then rubbed it up and down my wetness before entering me in one swift move of his hips.

I moaned as my eyes rolled back at the pure pleasure and the small bite of pain that his large engorged cock caused. I was so deliciously full of him... feeling every vein, every ridge. This man had been built for me, I knew that. We were completing each other.

He started to thrust fast and hard. He was in the mood for rough sex, and I didn't mind. I love my Dom rough and soft. I grabbed the bars of the headboard and wrapped my legs around his waist, raising my hips with his thrusts, loving how undone he became when he was in me.

"I'm gonna come, Dolcetta; you feel too good." He grunted tightly, his face buried in my neck.

"Come with me, Dolcetta," he commanded just before his thrusts turned more erratic as his hand trailed down between us and he started to rub my clit with his thumb.

I felt the orgasm come as a tidal wave of electricity and as he bit my neck, I came probably harder than I ever had. The orgasm was so powerful it was almost painful.

Dom followed quickly, roaring my name and emptying himself inside of me.

I realized as he lay heavily on top of me, his softening cock still in me, that it had to be the first time in my life I had sex without protection, and I didn't mind.

I sighed in contentment, enjoying his weight on me, his body in mine. I felt so at peace like that. I brought my hand up and gently stroked his hair as he softly kissed the top of my breast.

"Tonight was supposed to be about you, and you rocked my world," I said breathlessly, my heart still hammering in my chest.

He let out a low chuckle. "Trust me, Dolcetta, it was very much about me alright." He brushed the back of his hand along the curve of my breast. "Tasting you, being inside you, it's a marvel I'm addicted to." He kissed my nipple. "Te amo, Dolcetta."

"I love you too."

He groaned as he left my body, rolling to his side and taking me with him.

"I'm very grateful for tonight," he started, resting his forehead against mine. "But why did you do all that?"

"Because I wanted tonight to be special." I rested my hand on his cheek. "You are the love of my life, Domenico Romano. And I want to stay with you here. The good and bad doesn't matter. I know the man you are; I know your heart." I let my hand trail down from his cheek to his chest, on top of his heart. "I know you won't see it like that, but you were thirteen, Dom. You were still a child. You may see yourself as the perpetrator, but you were also a victim whether you like it or not."

"I could have—"

I leaned closer, kissing him to make him stop. "It does not matter. I'm here to stay."

He wrapped his arm tighter around me, pulling my body flush to his. "Are you sure? It won't be easy."

"I know. Cassie and Luca explained to me a lot of the rules, the obligations coming with loving a man like you."

"And?"

"You're worth that and so much more." I moved my leg to straddle his and felt his cock starting to swell against my lower stomach. "Already?"

He shrugged with a grin. "I'm Italian and you're my woman... what did you expect?"

"I need another minute; you drained me."

"Um, I can be patient. The other good thing, though, is not having to see Matteo."

"Actually, you do have to. We're expected tomorrow morning."

He pulled his head back a little. "We?"

"Luca arranged the meeting for me. I'm going to swear loyalty to the famiglia."

"Are you sure you want to do that now?" he asked, resting his hand on my hip, stroking his thumb back and forth on my naked skin. "It can wait for a month or two, you know. There's no rush."

"I know."

"Once you take the oath, it's over, you know. There's no turning back. The only way out is—"

"Death. Yes, I'm aware. Luca made it abundantly clear." I grabbed the hand that was on my hip and kissed his palm. "But I also know that it's already too late. There's a before Dom and a with Dom. I'm not inclined to try an 'after Dom.' Is it so hard to believe that I feel so deeply for you than you do for me?"

"Yes!" he exclaimed. "You're a dream come true, India. You're as stunning inside and out, patient, loving, smart, and a fucking bomb in bed. How can I not be crazy about you?"

"Yes, and for me, you are the most beautiful man. You are gentle and loyal and so funny."

"Don't forget to mention my cock."

I laughed. "How could I forget this gigantic piece of man?" I ran my hand down and grabbed it, my fingers far from touching around his girth. "You're stretching me so deliciously. I never want another cock inside of me."

"And you never will," he muttered before taking my mouth in another passionate kiss. "Now let me remind you yet again how deliciously my cock is stretching you."

———

The next morning I woke Dom up with a blow job and breakfast in bed.

Seeing him so happy made me feel complete. I'd never felt anything like that before this sense of belonging with someone.

We almost ended up late for our meeting with Matteo because Dom had been adamant to make me come when we were in the shower and I could never say no to his wicked tongue and mouth.

Just the thought of them made me tingle between the legs.

I sighed at the memory, pressing my thighs together as we drove to Matteo's house.

Dom rested a possessive hand on my thigh, sliding his fingers between my thighs.

"I told Luca we'll be staying here another night, Dolcetta… I intend to take you on every flat surface of the condo."

"I'll hold you to that."

He squeezed my thigh in a silent promise just as we crossed the gates to Matteo's place.

"This place looks much more like a military compound than a home," I commented as we passed a gray concrete building.

"Yes, I think he wants it like that. He sees himself like the head of the army…" Dom cocked his head to the side. "Which in retrospect is exactly what it is."

I nodded. I knew it would be a steep learning curve, but Dom was worth it.

"Are you sure?" he asked once again as we parked

in front of the only building that actually looked like a house. "Once you do it—"

I leaned on my seat and stopped him with a kiss. "Yes, I'm sure. Now let's go."

I got out of the car before he had the opportunity to question me again. It would take a while for him to accept it was my choice and that he was worth it, but I had the patience for it.

The silent majordomo opened the door and led us silently down the house.

The silence and dark, old furniture gave this house an ominous look that was oppressive. It really felt like the walls were full of secrets.

"D-D-Dom, I-India, h-how are y-you d-d-doing?"

I smiled at the tall, lanky young man behind the desk. I remember him taking Jude to the chess tournament and I liked him from the start. He was such a broken, soft boy and part of me was eager to help him, and I hoped that he would one day trust me enough to talk to me.

I smiled at him. "Enzo, I'm so pleased to see you again. I'm doing very well. How are you?"

He nodded with a smile. "I'm o-okay. Ma-Mateo said you're j-j-joining the f-f-famiglia. I'm h-happy."

Dom wrapped his arm around my waist. "Don't try to steal my woman, Enzo. I'll keep my eyes on you."

Enzo's smile ticked and he froze just a little, not enough for Dom to notice but enough for me.

He turned his eyes toward me, and his demeanor changed immediately as if he knew I knew.

"M-Matteo is waiting f-for you," he said, pointing to the door.

I shook my head, concentrating on the matter ahead. I would discuss Enzo with Dom later.

We entered an office that was a true representation of his owner, all black and glass... cold, calculated. It was Matteo Genovese.

"You didn't change your mind," he enunciated mockingly as soon as we walked in. "I'm not sure if it makes you brave or foolish."

"It makes me 'in love.'"

"Ah." He nodded, taking a drag of his big cigar. "Foolish then, good to know."

Dom rolled his eyes. "You know why we're here. Could we just move along?"

"Of course, *brother*." Matteo smirked as Dom's nostrils flared in frustration. That man was the king of shit stirrers.

Matteo turned toward me. "You've decided to join the famiglia?"

"Yes."

He took a drag of his cigar. "Did Domenico explain to you what it means? Once you swear your loyalty, you're in... only your death will free you."

"I'm aware."

He put his cigar down in his ashtray and jerked his head toward me.

I cleared my throat. *"Giuro fedeltà alla famiglia. Giuro di rispettare le regole e proteggere i segreti del nostro sangue. io sono la famiglia."* I swear loyalty to the family. I swear to respect the rules and protect the secrets of our blood. I am the family.

I quickly glanced at Dom who winked at me. I aced it.

Matteo looked at Dom for a few seconds, his face thoughtful. He could make it harder for me if he wanted to. Luca had told me that he could ask for a proof of my loyalty which may include murder if he so desired. But Matteo simply sighed before standing up and walking up to me.

He rested his hands on my shoulders. *"Benvenuta nella famiglia,"* he said before kissing both of my cheeks, then turning to Dom and kissing him too.

When Dom came toward me and grabbed my hand, I turned toward him. *"Lo giuro su Dio e sulla famiglia. Il mio cuore, il mio amore e la mia lealtà sono tuoi. Ora e per sempre. Faccio questo giuramento col sangue, nel silenzio della notte, e sotto la luce delle stelle e lo splendore della luna. Tutti i tuoi segreti saranno miei, tutti i tuoi peccati saranno miei, tutto il tuo dolore sarà mio. Sono tuo completamente."*

This was the vows that Cassie had given at her wedding to Luca. It was the strongest promise you could ever make in the famiglia. It was my promise to give myself completely to him.

Dom looked away, blinking rapidly, fighting back tears at my oath.

Matteo rolled his eyes, pointing his forefinger from Dom to me. "*Sposala.*"

Dom brought my hand to his lips and kissed the back of it. "I'm planning on it."

Matteo helped himself to a glass of scotch before going back around his desk. "Now that's done, Domenico, I need to speak with you." He turned to me. "Go wait in the lounge. Enzo can give you a drink."

"Of course." I knew better than to question his command, especially only minutes after swearing my allegiance to him.

Dom leaned down and gave me a quick kiss. "I won't be long."

"Take your time."

Enzo stood up as soon as I exited the room.

"They have to chat for a while," I said after closing the door behind me.

"Y-y-you w-ant something to drink?" he asked, coming toward me.

I shook my head with a smile, studying him. He had the black hair and eyes that were trademarks of the famiglia, but his skin was so pale, almost translucent, and despite being in his twenties, he didn't look older than fifteen.

He was the kind of person we wanted to protect but who would refuse showing any more weakness…

"What do you say we play a game while we wait?" I asked him, pointing at the beautiful wooden chess board at the side of the room.

Enzo studied me for a couple of seconds before nodding. It had to be tiring to always be on your guard like that. Was it a Mafia thing, to always be on high alert?

"This is stunning." I ran my hand on the board sculpted directly on the table.

He nodded again and it made me sad for him. He was clearly limiting his verbal communication because of his stuttering, and he didn't know me well enough to trust me.

"White or black?"

He sat at the black side, silently replying to my question and allowing me to start.

"I'm not very good at this," I admitted after playing for about five minutes. I grimaced and looked at all the pieces he'd already taken.

"I am good," he simply replied, taking my tower. "Check."

I twisted my mouth to the side. I was not very good for sure, but I never thought I was that bad either.

I moved a pawn, taking the one that made me check. "Jude really loves chess. He enjoys spending time with you."

"J-Jude is d-d-different. He und-derstands."

"Understands what?"

Enzo threw me a knowing look, as if he were onto me and he was not a fool. He looked down to the board again. "That y-you should n-n-never underestimate an adv-v-versary just b-because he l-l-looks weaker." He let out a big sigh after struggling with this long sentence. "Checkmate." He stood up. "I have w-w-ork now. G-g-good game."

I watched him walk back to his desk.

Good game? The kid beat me in seven minutes flat.

He had a very sharp, quick mind. No wonder Matteo kept him close; he was brilliant.

I needed to know more about him; he was intriguing. Maybe I could ask Luca to invite him over when Jude would be back from his break.

Enzo was a challenge I wanted to conquer.

18

DOM

"What is it you want?" I asked Matteo, crossing my arms on my chest.

He arched his eyebrows, pointing at his chest. "Me? *Vai*! You're the one whining like a little bitch because I killed that man."

"Yes, a man whom I wanted to talk to. A man who didn't deserve to die."

He tapped his forefinger on his desk. "This is your weakness, Domenico, yours and Gianluca. You can't lead this life and have a conscience. You can deny it as much as you want but you can't." He shook his head. "If I let that man go after what he did to you. It would have been a liability to have him free again and what would my men say if I didn't avenge you? They would think I didn't have their backs. That man had to die."

"It had nothing to do with you. His grief was not against the famiglia. His grudge was against me. I hurt his family, and he wanted revenge. I'm sure that you of all people can understand that."

He nodded. "I do understand and I can also empathize."

"You don't know what that word means."

He threw me an exasperated look but ignored my comment. "But you have to understand that even disregarding the famiglia, this man hurt my family, my blood, and this can't be left unpunished." He took a deep breath. "I made his death as painless as I could."

Knowing how Matteo loved to play with his victims... how he enjoyed their screams, I knew that killing him painlessly had been a great act of kindness for him.

He lit a cigarette and extended the pack toward me with his gold Zippo.

Oh, the hell with this, I deserved one. I grabbed the pack and lit a cigarette too.

"Plus, I find it quite ironic that you are judging me when you went out of your way, all the way to Canada, to hurt a man."

I kept my face emotionless.

"I don't—"

He raised his hand to stop me and rolled his eyes. "Don't lie to me, *idiota*. I had a call from Fabrizio, asking for a favor."

Fucking Fabrizio!

"I told him to contact Luca or me when he wanted me to pay him back."

Matteo chuckled. "Maybe you did, but what he wants, only I can grant him." He puffed out his chest a little.

"You love having all the power, don't you?"

He gave me a half smile. "I worked enough for it."

And I knew what he was not saying. He'd sacrificed enough for it.

"What I don't get is why you didn't simply have him killed? Much less messy and who is that guy? He is an architect or something."

"He was India's ex. He hurt my woman."

Matteo shrugged. "Before she was yours? I don't see how that is punishable."

He couldn't understand. Matteo barely felt anything on his best days and he lived and breathed by Mafia's rules.

"It is to me."

"And why just disable him? Killing him would have been much easier."

"He needs to learn what it's like to be diminished, weak, to be at the mercy of others."

"Oh!" Matteo's smile turned wicked. "I think there may be hope for you after all, brother."

No matter how unfair it was and how much it reopened the wounds of my sins, I needed to know more about that man and how he had chased me.

"Tell me more about the man, Emily's brother… Who was he?"

"Why?" Matteo took a drag of his cigarette. "It won't help you."

"I deserve to know."

"Deserve…" Matteo cocked his head to the side. "Since when do we get what we deserve in life?" He let out a little humorless laugh. "You can't be that naïve, Domenico; you've been around long enough. And you know what I deserve? Not cleaning up behind you and Gianluca, not trying to find stupid excuses because I let you both bend the rules over and over again."

"It's because we're your favorites."

Matteo rolled his eyes. "Blood will only get you so far, Domenico. Don't forget your place or misuse my leniency toward you."

It felt weird to hear him admit it somehow, that he was treating us differently—mostly because I was his brother.

"Tell me, please."

He let out a sigh of exasperation. "His name was Daniel. He received your details by mail and decided to follow you around. He didn't know what exactly you were. He only thought you ran a prostitution ring."

"I see."

"No, I don't think you do. If you'd talked to me instead of ignoring what was happening, you wouldn't have been hurt and he wouldn't have had to die."

"I didn't think it was that important; I thought I could handle it."

"Indeed, you did. And see how it turned out."

I rolled my eyes. "Is that why you wanted me to stay behind? To chastise me like a petulant child?"

"No, there's no reason for me to do that. You think I'm the devil and you think you know best." He shrugged. "I need you to help me clean up this mess because it's as important for you as it is for me."

I knew I would help him because even if he was an asshole, I owed him that much but it didn't mean I couldn't taunt him in the process. "I'm not the one in charge; I've got nothing to lose."

"Don't you?" He nodded. "So far, the rat played with Benny and Savio's head to kill Luca, had them kidnap his woman and tried to kill you. Don't you see what all they have in common?"

Luca, that was who.

Matteo nodded at the look on my face. "Helping me is helping yourself."

It was a bit of a stretch, but at the same time, how could I say no? He could so easily order me if he wanted to.

"I'll do anything for Luca."

Matteo smirked. "You're making me feel so fuzzy inside."

"Luca told me about the list you have."

"We need to work through it, and we need to do it soon."

"Why?

He looked away and I saw his jaw tick as his nostrils flared. "The Italians are coming."

Fuck! This year was the worst for this. After all the changes, all the rules we bent.

Luca, marrying outside the family, taking me as consigliere. Matteo making a deal with the Russians.

Despite being a sociopathic asshole, I couldn't help but feel a certain kinship to him. Was it due to our blood relationship? It was probably the case. I didn't have any family—not a blood one anyway—and somehow, I didn't want him gone. Another king would not accept what he accepted.

"When are they coming? Why are they coming? Aren't you the one usually going there for the yearly meetings?"

"Yes, but…" He paused, his jaw ticking again.

Matteo was hiding something and it made me curious because whatever it was, Matteo was the master of keeping his face smooth. Whatever he was hiding was affecting him deeply for him to show even the smallest sign on his face. It had to be juicy and it would be good ammunition to have against him—just in case.

"I have not been able to join for the past few years."

"I see." Mateo was not an avoider; after all, he enjoyed confrontation and drama.

"So they decided to make it easy and come here." He pinched the bridge of his nose. "We need this."

We needed the rat to make up for that and keep the Italians occupied while they were here. There was no two ways about that.

"What do you need?" I asked finally, no longer being an asshole to him. He clearly had a lot on his plate too. I could cut him some slack for once.

He looked at me with incredulity, as if he couldn't believe I was giving in. "Mostly? Your time."

I wasn't sure what he meant by 'mostly,' but with India waiting for me in the other room, I didn't want to spend more time here than was necessary. "Okay, when do we start?"

"We're not starting right now." He looked down at the phone on his desk and scrolled through it. "I have a few things to do now."

I shrugged. "I can help." I mostly wanted to know what secret he was hiding for me.

He gave me a half smile. "Be careful, brother. I might start to think you care about me."

I rolled my eyes.

He waved his hand toward the door. "Just enjoy your woman, celebrate your engagement or whatever this was, marry her, start to procreate. Enjoy it while you can."

That was again oddly caring for the sociopathic Mafia king.

"Be careful, Genovese. I might start to think you care about me," I teased, mimicking his earlier words.

"Who said I didn't?" he asked challengingly.

My jaw went slack with surprise. He had to be fucking with me. Yeah, there was no other choice. The only person Matteo Genovese cared about was Matteo Genovese.

"Mat—"

"Just go now. I'm done with you," he ordered dismissively, opening his laptop and starting to type away.

A new wave of indignation filled me at his rude dismissal. He could go fuck himself for all I cared.

I stood up stiffly and walked to the door.

"Oh, and Domenico?" he started as I touched the handle.

I turned my head, looking at him silently.

"Next time I call you? Pick up the fucking phone."

"Understood," I replied with the same cold tone before exiting the room.

I tried to not look as annoyed as I felt when I came out of the room but the concern in her eyes showed I didn't fool her. Of course I didn't; this woman was so attuned to me it was surreal.

"See you soon, *topolino*," I told Enzo before reaching for her hand.

"See you soon!" India called as I pulled her out of the room.

"You're okay?" she whispered as we walked down the corridor.

"Yes," I muttered. "It's just Matteo playing his little boss game and using the 'I saved your life' card."

"What did he want?"

I stopped and turned toward her; I had to share. If recent experiences taught me anything, it was to share. "He wanted me to hunt the rat."

19

DOM

My phone beeped and I cursed, looking down at Marco who was laughing from my bed.

Office now or I'll kill your brother.

"Your father is an asshole," I grumbled, grabbing the baby and putting him in the baby carrier on my chest before going down to the office.

The three girls were in the greenhouse, and I had wanted to spend some bonding time with my godson... something I was going to regret very dearly in the next few minutes.

I walked into the office to see Luca standing beside the window behind his desk and Matteo sitting on the leather chair across from him.

Luca turned toward me and rolled his eyes. "Really, Dom, again?"

I looked down at the little boy strapped at my chest. I dressed him just like I was dressed in a black faux leather jacket, a white t-shirt, black jeans, and combat boots, and a black wig that mimicked my hairdo.

I shrugged, trying to avoid Matteo's eyes. "It was my time with him, and I was supposed to be free for another hour." I finally looked toward Matteo who was looking from Marco to me like I was demented.

"It's just for fun. I—" I sighed.

Matteo shook his head. "Get your woman pregnant; make your own children clinically insane."

Getting India pregnant, I'd be lying if I said I didn't think about it. Of course I did. I imagined her full with our child, but it was still much too early. She'd only committed to me a month ago; she needed time.

"Why are you already here?"

He leaned back on his seat and smirked. "I missed you, brother."

I turned to Luca. I had no time for his games today.

Luca looked at his son again and threw me an exasperated look. I knew it annoyed him when I dressed up the little dude, and I think that was half the fun for me.

"Matteo spoke with Sebastiano Visconti. He agreed to let us come and have a chat with Sergio."

I raised an eyebrow and looked at Matteo, a little impressed.

Sebastiano Visconti was the head of the Vegas Mafia... In line to become the boss of the West Coast Mafia soon and he was usually very defensive of his territory and the men falling under it.

"What do you have on him?" I asked Matteo.

He let out a short laugh. "Ah, brother, you know me so well."

I wanted to remind him yet again not to call me that, but he already knew how much I hated it, and I was sure he was doing it just to annoy me. I guess being assholes did run in our genes.

"And what does it have to do with me?"

"I need you to come to Vegas tomorrow."

"No." I shook my head. *Fuck this shit!* I had plans with India! I was finally going to take her to the cabin. I had an engagement ring and everything. "I've got plans."

Matteo rolled his eyes. "Don't get your panties up in a bunch. Take your girl and make a weekend of it."

"I made a commitment." Or at least I was about to, and India was really looking forward to this trip.

Matteo snorted. "*Che e solo un modo stravagante per dire che sei uno zerbino del cazzo.*"

"Yes, I'm pussy-whipped and so what?" I challenged him.

Matteo sighed. "Fine, Gianluca. We're leaving at ten."

Luca nodded, taking a sip of the drink in his hand.

I raised my hand. "Wait a minute. What does that mean? Can't we just take a break? We've already ruled out four names on the list, Matteo. I—"

"And I told you before, we need to keep the momentum going. Once he knows we're getting closer, he'll be ready." He started to twist his signet ring around his finger. "And who told you you could question my orders? I killed men for much less."

It was my turn to smirk at him. "But you wouldn't kill your *brother*, would you?"

"Don't overestimate the loyalty I have to my blood."

If I were honest, I didn't even think he had any type of loyalty other than for the rules. "I would never."

He stood up. "Luca, tomorrow, ten at the airfield," he commanded.

Fuck me sideways! I couldn't let Luca leave for the weekend! The twins needed their dad, and I knew how anxious it was making him to leave them behind.

"Fuck it," I grumbled. "I'll do it, but I'm taking India, and please don't act like a psycho when she's around, okay?"

"I'll try my best," he replied dryly before looking

down at Marco in my arms. "And stop messing up the future capo. See you tomorrow." He exited the room.

I removed the wig from Marco's head and sat on the chair Matteo had just vacated.

"I'm not messing him up."

Luca took his seat across the desk. "I'm not sure, man... Just be grateful Matteo was not here when you dressed up *my son* as Carmen Miranda last week."

I shrugged, looking at the dozing little boy on my chest. "I wanted to give him options."

Luca shook his head. "You're lucky it made my wife laugh to tears or I swear I would have shot you in the kneecaps."

"Yeah," I leaned back on the seat with a weary sigh.

"You wanted to ask her to marry you this weekend, didn't you?"

Was I really that transparent? I nodded "And you know the cabin was the perfect location. If she said no, I could have just thrown myself from the nearby cliff."

"You're so dramatic. And let me tell you with how she is looking at you? How I caught her and my wife giggling?" He smiled. "There's no way she'd say no to you."

My heart sped up with elation at the thought. "I hope you're right."

"I know I am and Matteo's right." He pointed at his son asleep in his baby carrier. "Make your own and mess that one up. This one is mine to traumatize."

I laughed. "Duly noted. I'll be working on that soon."

Luca took a sip, his face returning to his serious business demeanor. "Thank you for doing it. I appreciate it."

"I don't mind doing it for you, Luca; you know that. It's just that Matteo is too pushy... even hasty, and I just think he could slow down a bit."

Luca looked away, chewing on his bottom lip. "I don't think he can though. He's not saying it but there are a few rumors running rampant within the ranks. The traitor nickname 'Mano Vendicativa' is being whispered and Matteo fears once his authority is questioned, he will be replaced."

I grimaced at that. It was true; being questioned was never great. Take away the fear and what does he have left?

"No matter how psycho he is, he has always been more or less good to us. Maybe it's because of the blood ties; maybe it's something else." Luca shrugged. "All I know is that I don't want another Italian meddling in our business."

"I know."

"And nothing is stopping you from asking her to marry you in Vegas."

I grimaced. "That's a bit tacky."

"It doesn't have to be. All that matters is who you're asking and how you feel." He pointed his fingers toward the greenhouse. "I asked Cassie to marry me after her kidnapping, while she was in bed. Not ideal and yet…"

"Yes." I stood up. "I'll think about it."

"Dom?" he called after I turned around to leave.

"Yeah?"

"Could I please get my son back?"

"Oh yeah." I let out a chuckle as I freed Marco from the baby carrier. "Be honest though, he is really cute like that."

"Maybe…" he admitted reluctantly.

"Okay, I'm going to tell India that plans have changed. Wish me luck."

"You don't need luck; the woman loves you."

"Yeah, and if it doesn't work, my magical penis will fix it."

"Dom, *per l'amor di Dio!*"

"That's basically what she says too when—"

Luca raised his left hand. "And we're done here."

I looked at him, cradling Marco lovingly against his chest, and felt the need again. I wanted babies with India. I wanted all of that. Now I just needed to see if she wanted it too. It was a big decision to have children within the Mafia. Our kids, just as Luca and Cassie's kids, would never be free, not really, and I knew India would be concerned about that. How could she not?

I found them in the greenhouse talking to Arabella about the plants they were taking care of.

"Sorry to interrupt girl time." I winked at India who had a pair of shears in her hand.

I loved how her face lit up when she saw me. It made my heart stall in my chest every time and I still had a hard time believing how much she loved me. Even with all the darkness, even knowing all of my sins, she still loved me.

"Do you mind if I kidnap India for a minute?"

Cassie laughed, gesturing me away. "No, you can have her but bring her back, okay?"

I looked at India walking toward me, swaying her hips a little more than necessary. "I can't promise you that." And it was not a lie. I was going to take her south by the wooded area in the garden, protected from prying eyes. I could probably sweet-talk her into a quickie against a tree.

"You're canceling our weekend," she said matter-of-factly just as we started down the path.

I turned toward her briskly. I didn't expect her to guess so easily.

I grabbed her hand, intertwining our fingers together. I just had to touch her when I was near her; there was no other way.

"I saw Matteo arrive. I know better than to think it was for some brotherly time."

I leaned against her and nudged her playfully. "I'm sorry."

She pulled our hands up and kissed the back of mine. "Don't be, I understand. Just promise me to be careful."

"I'm going to Vegas. I want you to come with me."

She stopped walking and turned toward me, her face barely hiding her excitement. "Are you sure? I don't want to be a hindrance and I'm not angry, I swear."

I leaned down and kissed her softly. "You're not a hindrance, and I know you won't be angry. You're so understanding it's ridiculous. I want you there with me..." I pulled her toward me, wrapping my arms around her waist. "What I need to do won't take too long. And then it's you and me hitting town, what do you say?"

She smiled at me. "Of course I'll come. I've never been to Vegas. Maybe I can go see a male stripper show while I wait for you."

I shook my head. "Nope, Dolcetta. I can strip for you, it's as much of a stripper you'll see."

She rubbed at my chest over my shirt. "Jealous."

"Very much so."

"You're the only one for me, Domenico Romano. No Channing Tatum lookalike will ever be able to change that."

"A lookalike?"

"Yeah, because for the real deal? All bets are off," she replied cheekily.

I trailed my nose along her jawline. "Ah, man, I now have to go hunt for Channing Tatum."

She laughed, wrapping her arms around my neck. "I love you, silly man."

I cradled her cheek with my hand, I would never get tired of hearing her say that. "I love you too, Dolcetta, *più della mia stessa vita.*"

And it was true; I did love her more than my life, more than my vows to the famiglia, and that was dangerous; I knew it.

She was my religion, my commitment, my everything.

I thought about the ring in my room. Maybe Luca was right. It didn't really matter where I asked her to marry me. Yep, that was what I'd do. This weekend I'd ask India McKenna to be my wife.

EPILOGUE
ONE

DOM

"One more drink," Matteo offered, extending two shot glasses toward me and Sergio.

I looked at my watch once more. It was so much harder to get him drunk than we expected and even the drugs Matteo put in his drink about fifteen minutes ago were still not working.

Sergio was a fat man; maybe we didn't use enough. Part of me almost wanted Matteo to grab him and take him to a basement somewhere to get the information and be done with it.

I knew he couldn't. He would have been the first to do it if he could, but torturing our men, even the former ones, without any proof would raise questions we didn't particularly want to answer.

I threw another look at my watch, getting a

warning glare from Matteo, but I didn't much care. I was supposed to be back at the hotel over forty minutes ago. I'd booked it all, couples' massage, a show, and the proposal, and this fucking job was once again ruining things. I couldn't warn India either. This bar had no reception. It was on purpose, of course, but now I had no way to tell her I would be late.

I sighed, pretending to sip the drink.

"What's up with you?"

Matteo's nostrils flared; he was not happy with me, but I didn't care.

I shrugged, looking down at my now-empty glass, pouting like a five-year-old.

"Our boy is in love with a girl with a gold-plated vagina... He just doesn't like leaving her alone in case she gets her common sense back and leaves him behind." Matteo explained, his voice dripping with sarcasm.

I sent him a withering look as Sergio let out a booming laugh. "How come you came all the way to Vegas? You always said it was too flashy for you."

Matteo shrugged. "Checking on the famiglia... Making sure they remember where their loyalty lies. Remind them that it's not because they have left us that they are not to keep our secrets."

"Che?"

"Remember where your wife comes from Sergio. You talk, we talk."

His eyes widened, understanding what Matteo was saying. "What? I…" He shook his head. "That's not a part of my life I ever want to get out." He threw me a quick glance. "No offense."

I looked away. Why would I take offense? I had been just a boy at the time; he was the one who 'broke' one of the girls and decided to keep her.

He was the grown man who kept a sixteen-year-old girl as a gift from my father. The fact that they were still married two decades later didn't matter.

He looked at us, his pupils a little dilated—the drugs were finally working. He would wake up in the morning with a hazy brain as if he had a hangover and not many memories of what we discussed.

"I regret some things… I left because of all that. To start fresh. It is not to talk about it now. As far as I'm concerned it never happened."

Matteo threw me an exasperated look. It was clear that he was not lying, and it was also clear we wasted our time here.

"Bene, that's the way it should be," Matteo replied, taking a drink now.

After a few minutes of idle chatter, Matteo tapped his hand on the table. "It was nice catching up with you, Sergio, but I need to go now. I've got dinner with Sebastiano."

"Ah, si." The older man wiped some sweat from his forehead with the back of his shirt sleeve. "We are good, si?"

He was nervous; of course, he was, because no matter what rumor may be rampant in the famiglia ranks, everyone knew that Matteo was a heartless sociopath, and everyone knew what his basement was all about.

Matteo stood up and adjusted the cuffs of his shirt. "We are and as long as you keep your mouth shut, we will be."

"*Siempre.*"

Matteo looked at me. "Andiamo."

"I'm not coming to dinner with you," I muttered as we exited the bar. "I've got plans."

He rolled his eyes, lighting a cigar as soon as we stepped outside. "Calm your tits. You're not invited. It's a capo dinner. You're barely a consigliere."

Did he think he was insulting me? I couldn't care less about ranks. I took the position to be close to my best friend and make sure he was safe; the rest didn't matter.

"A consigliere with royal blood, no?" I replied just to piss him off.

He blew the smoke right in my face. "Go to your woman, Domenico. Let the actual men deal with things."

Once again if he was trying to rail me, it was an epic fail. Going to my woman was all that mattered, and if it made me less of a man in his eyes, I couldn't care less.

My phone vibrated multiple times in my pocket,

announcing an inflow of messages that had been waiting for some reception.

I got it out of my pocket and noticed seven texts from India plus a voicemail. I was truly fucked.

Matteo started to say something, but I ignored him, twirling around and going up the strip to our hotel as fast as I could while reading the texts India sent.

Where are you? Couple massage is in ten. Love you.

Dom, are you okay? We missed our appointment.

Domenico Romano, you better be dead.

No, don't be dead. I don't mean that. Love you.

I smiled at the screen despite the anxiety. Even angry she couldn't properly be mean.

Five more minutes and I'm going to see male strippers. Your fault.

Fine, I'm going, I'll see you when I see you.

The next text was simply a photo of a stage with half-naked men. I was going to kill them, yep all of them.

I listened to the voicemail as I entered the lobby of the Bellagio.

"I can't do this anymore," she said with a small voice.

No, no, no, no. She couldn't just give up on us. That was stupid. I swiped my card in the elevator and pressed our floor.

Fuck it, fuck all of it! Just the thought of not being with her was unbearable. She had to forgive me. She loved me; I loved her. She knew my life would never be easy. I could not always put her first, but she ought to know that I always would when the choice was mine.

I was going to retrieve that ring and I was going to find her and ask her to marry me. I would make her understand that without her, there wouldn't be a *me*.

She was my light, my breath, my life. I existed for her only, and that taking herself away from me would be a death sentence. I was not even being dramatic; it was true. That day when I saw her at the airport, it was the beginning of the end for me.

Yes, she'll understand, she loves you, I tried to reassure myself as I opened the door of the suite and froze on the threshold.

The whole living space was lit with dozens of candles, soft music in the background, and a bucket with a bottle of champagne.

I frowned, taking a couple of tentative steps into the room, closing the door softly.

"Dolcetta?"

"I love you, Domenico," she said as she appeared from the bedroom, dressed in a stunning off-the-shoulder flowy red dress.

The vise in my chest settled in a second, and I had to blink away the tears of relief at having her here with me.

"You scared me, really," I admitted, taking another step toward her.

She raised her hand to stop me in my tracks.

"Did you really think I was going to walk away from us?" She shook her head. "You still seem unable to see how deeply I love you. Is it because you don't think you're worthy? Maybe but it's okay, I'll make you understand that you are, even if it takes a lifetime."

"A lifetime with you is all I'm asking for," I said in an almost begging tone.

She smiled. "That's good because…" She got on one knee and the world around me stopped. "Domenico Romano, will you marry me?"

I looked down at her completely dumbfounded. Of all the things I expected to happen, this was not one of them. I was supposed to do that; it was the plan. She couldn't… Finally I returned to my body and walked briskly to the bedroom.

"I'm not going to lie; that's not exactly the reaction I hoped for," she shouted from the living room.

I smiled at that as I retrieved the small black box from my travel bag. It was going to be a mutual proposal, which was so uncommon, but to be fair, everything between us was from the start. It was somehow logical for our proposal to be unconventional.

I walked back into the room where she was still waiting for me on one knee and stopped right in front of her, my hand wrapped around the box tightly.

She looked up at me, her eyes full of confusion but also trust. Her faith in me was so humbling.

I copied her gesture and knelt in front of her.

"I really thought you left me," I admitted. "All that because I know I don't deserve you. I know that, and yet I want you, all of you, and I know you think I'm enough, Lord knows why, but I still want to be a better man for you. Getting as close as possible to the man you deserve." I showed her the box in my hand. "You stole my moment, Dolcetta. I wanted to do that."

"It's modern times, Domenico; a woman can propose."

I nodded. "She can but I don't deserve a woman like you kneeling at my feet."

She gave me a little seductive smile. "I don't remember you complaining when I knelt at your feet last night."

I grabbed her by the back of her neck and kissed her deeply. "No, and I never will," I whispered against her lips before pulling away a little and showing her the diamond and emerald engagement ring I bought her. "I'll marry you, India McKenna. I've wanted to marry you since the moment I kissed you. You're the love of my life, and just knowing you want to spend the rest of your life with me is baffling, humbling, and incredible all at once." I smiled, grabbing her hand. "So I'll ask you too. India McKenna, will you marry me?"

Her emerald eyes were filled with tears, and under the candlelight, it made them shine like the emerald on her ring. "Of course I'll marry you, Domenico. You're the best man in the world. You make me feel special, loved, safe... all at once. I never feel more beautiful than when I see myself through your eyes, and I never knew you could love someone as much as I love you. I never want to not feel like that ever again. You're my life too, you know."

I slid the ring on her finger and sealed the deal with a kiss.

"Let's get married now," she whispered against my lips.

I growled as my dick was starting to harden. I wanted her now, naked on the carpet and screaming my name as she wore my ring.

"No, not now. No eloping for us." I took her lips in another bruising kiss. "I want to have a real wedding. I want us to stand in front of Father Mario and swear our love. Show to all of them that you chose to love me. That it was a choice; that it was not an accident. That you truly want me."

India grabbed my face in her hands. "Okay, we will get married like Kate and William if it's what you want, and I'll shout it from every rooftop in the city if I need to. Domenico Romano is the love of my life, and I'm the luckiest woman in the world to have him love me too. How does that sound?"

I smirked, leaning on her slowly until she had her back on the floor and I was on top of her. "That sounds perfect." I trailed my hand up her leg and under her dress. "Now, *la mia futura moglie*, let me not only tell you how much I love you, but let me show you."

She smiled, wrapping my arms around my neck. "Yes, show me..."

And for the rest of the night, I showed her just how much I loved her.

EPILOGUE TWO

MATTEO

I rubbed my face, looking down at the list on my screen. Five down, seven to go.

The trip to Vegas had been a waste of time, and my dinner with Sebastiano had been as enjoyable as pins under my nails... I'd hated every second of it.

The rat didn't know it, but I was closing in on him. He grated on my nerves. He was so much smarter than I anticipated, and I hated that.

I was not used to being bested. At anything and this one, I just could not lose.

I fought too hard, gave up too much to be where I was now, to keep our rank straight, to inspire fear. It was not to have a punk try to ruin it all for me.

I leaned back on my seat. He was going to see what it was like when hellfire rained down on him. I would destroy him and everyone and everything that he may have cared for.

A feeling I was not used to hit me square in the chest... fear as I heard a ringtone I hoped I'd never hear.

I unlocked my last drawer and undid the double bottom to retrieve the flip burner phone I had there. Only one person had that number... the person protecting my most precious secret.

"Speak," I barked.

"They found her."

Fuck me! I closed my eyes, pinching the bridge of my nose. How was that possible? That rat bested me once more, and this time it was much worse because this was not only my title at risk. "Send her here."

"What are you going to do?"

I shook my head before resting it wearily against the headrest of my leather seat. "I'm going to tell her brother she exists and is on her way."

Matteo will come your way in the fall 2021!

AUTHOR'S NOTE

Thank you so much for reading Dom and India's story. I hope you enjoyed it as much as I enjoyed writing it.

Also, if you have it in your heart to leave a little review, I would be really grateful.

A few questions are still unanswered and there's a reason trust me – It is a series of three books and it will all be answered. Each book will concentrate on a different sexy Mafia man and his strong heroine.

Make sure to check **Cruel King**, the final book of **The Cosa Nostra** Series. It will be Matteo's book You don't want to miss it because Matteo is my favorite sociopath 😌. It will be released **October/November 2021**.

I wanted to thank my Street Team for always promoting my work. I appreciate you girls much more than you think.

I also wanted to thank my betas –Liz and Ashley for your enthusiasm about this series – It means a lot.

All the Best,
R.G. Angel xx

ABOUT ME

I'm a trained lawyer, world traveler, coffee addict, cheese aficionado, avid book reviewer and blogger.

I consider myself as an 'Eclectic romantic' as I love to devour every type of romance and I want to write romance in every sub-genre I can think of.

When I'm not busy doing all my lawyerly mayhem, and because I'm living in rainy (yet beautiful) Britain, I mostly enjoy indoor activities such as reading, watching TV, playing with my crazy puppies and writing stories I hope will make you dream and will bring you as much joy as I had writing them.

If you want to know any of the latest news join my reader group R.G.'s Angels on Facebook or subscribe to my newsletter!

Keep calm and read on!

R.G. Angel

ALSO, BY R.G. ANGEL

The Patricians series
Bittersweet Legacy
Bittersweet Revenge
Bittersweet Truth
Bittersweet Love (Coming soon)

The Cosa Nostra series
The Dark King (Prequel Novella)
Broken Prince

Standalones
Lovable
The Tragedy of Us
The Bargain

Printed in Great Britain
by Amazon